Shalom Boston

Dr. Benjamin Goodnick A"H

First published 2018

Published by

TARGUM PUBLISHERS

Shlomo ben Yosef 131a/1
Jerusalem 9380581
editor@targumpublishers.com

Distributed by

BOOKS & BEYOND WHOLESALE

211 Elaine St
Lakewood N.J. 08701
732-668-1304
booksandbeyond2@gmail.com

Printed in Israel

To My Father, My Guide, My Role Model,
Who Brought Us All Closer to Hashem:

Benjamin Goodnick, Dov Ben Zechariah Tzvi A"H

His Morals, His Favorite Sayings:

"The Virtue of Adversity" to Help Us To Grow from Those Times

That Hashem's Blessings May Not Seem that Way,

"The Attitude of Gratitude" To Always Be Ready

To Thank Hashem for Everything, Everything From a Parking
Place to A Shidduch

To Care About All People: Including Those Who Have Yet to
Appreciate True Closeness to Hashem and Walk in His Ways

To Always Be Ready to Show Love to All Others But Especially To
Our People, Our Friends, Our Loved Ones

And To Always Work to Come Closer to Hashem For Everything
And To Show It in Our Good Deeds and Most of All in Our
Davening

That Should Brook No Interruptions in Our Direct Conversation
With Hashem, Above & Beyond All Others, Whose Creations,
Even at their Very Best, Are a Combination of Earth, Blood, and
Soul.

May His Merits Always Be A Blessing for My Family, My Friends
and the People of Israel.

And May Moshiach Come Without Further Delay.

Pesach Yoel (Paul Joel) Goodnick
November 29, 2017

CONTENTS

PROLOGUE

Shalom, Yerushalayim. Good-bye. I won't be seeing you for a long time. I don't want to go but I have to. I don't know how to convince my mother to stay.

"Shoshi," Imma said to me a few days ago, "It's done. We're going to Harvard University in the United States. They accepted me." The words burst like a lightning flash and a thunderbolt at the same instant – right over my head. I was stunned. I could not move or speak.

Imma had talked about going. All at once it was real. We were leaving Yerushalayim. I cried and cried but it didn't make any difference to her.

She had no pity. My mother was changing my life forever. Because Abba left her and she's all alone doesn't mean I have to lose my friends, too. It wasn't my fault they got divorced. I know that's not the real reason we're going. Imma has to find work to make a living for both of us. Abba isn't giving her any money. He says he needs what he makes for himself. So she's going where they offered her a job – a very good job, Imma says. So I have to lose out. I suppose it's going to be "Shalom, Boston."

Imma says it's beautiful at Harvard and an honor to be chosen to teach there. How should I know? And I really don't care; my friends are here. They come first. I may never see my friends – or Abba – again. But I'm not giving up. I'm going to fight all the way – even after I get to America.

I

FAREWELL PARTY

W ell, were you surprised?" My mother asked as she
opened the door after my loud pounding.

"I was speechless. I just couldn't believe it. It was
wonderful! Look at these two bags full of gifts that I dragged here.
I can barely lift them off the ground."

"Let me help you, and I'd like to hear all about the party. I hope
you're not tired, though," she smiled, "because I'll need your help.
You know we have to take our luggage over tonight. Do you want
a snack first?"

"No, Imma, I'm not at all hungry. They made sure they fed me
well at the farewell party. I feel stuffed."

"All right, then, we can save time. Let's finish packing. We're
nowhere near done and have lots to do before we're on our way.
And I can see you're going to have stuffed suitcases."

I got back to my packing, but I couldn't concentrate. Inside I felt lost
and lonesome. The"bubble had burst." My excitement was all over.

The memories of the party were still so real. I needed to keep
them fresh and never forget them.

* * *

My friends were laughing and talking, shouting and singing, and playing games all over the room. My eyes blinked; they began to tear and couldn't stop.

I turned back to the "farewell" cake in the middle of the long table covered with a white cotton cloth decorated with flowers. Ednah and her mother had baked a cake in my honor. I had been so surprised – almost shrieked – when Daniela and Rahel marched in holding it high on their fingertips and plopped it right in front of me. The girls sang a song they made up with the title "Shalom Yerushalayim, Shalom Boston." Eva, the artist in our sixth-grade class, had printed the words in white on the pink icing.

The girls had taken so many pictures for me. Some were with each of my friends and then with the whole bunch of us together. Others were of me blowing out the large white and pink twined candle in the center of the cake, cutting the slices and taking my first mouthful. Everyone was so excited.

Meira made me feel sad and happy at the same time. It was funny the way she made sure she sat or stood close to me when our photos were snapped because "I want to see you always near me."

I made them promise to send me the photos as soon as they were ready. I would need them for the memories to keep me warm. But I would have to write to them first so they would know where to mail them.

Now they were crowding about watching me quietly, bright-eyed and smiling while my nervous hands reached for the heap of parting gifts on the table. I was all thumbs as I struggled to take apart the ribbons and wrappings.

And I have no idea how they were able to save the money to buy me all those gifts.

* * *

"Shoshi, you're back peering out the window. Must I keep checking on you? We've got lots to do yet. Finish your suitcase."

My eyes and cheeks were moist. I reached up to touch the half of the gold *Mizpah* charm Dvorah had given me. I could see her fingering her half and feeling as I did. We had read together the verse from the Bible and cried over it before separating the charm into its two parts – "The Lord watch between me and thee while we are absent from one another." We kissed and hugged and cried on each other's shoulder and swore eternal friendship.

I had always admired Dvorah's bright curly hair, her wide-open, laughing hazel eyes and warm embrace. Dvorah really liked people. I was lucky to have her for my best friend; being with her made me feel happy.

A little bronze key fell to the floor as I unwrapped my next gift. It was a beautiful red leather diary with so many empty pages waiting for me to fill. I had looked at Tzippy and smiled. I was sure it was her present; she knows how much I like to write. In school we passed notes and giggled over the short stories and silly poems we made up.

"Thank you so much. You'll never know how much this diary means to me."

No one will know what's in my diary; it will be only for my eyes. I hugged it tightly. My diary will be close and dear to my heart, to confide and share my secret thoughts and feelings.

I spread out the rest of my gifts on the floor: all kinds of colored stationery, pen and pencil sets, lots of barrettes, bows and earrings and one manicure set, and the stuffed donkeys and bears and hearts, feeling so soft against my cheek. And there were so many more... How would I fit them all in my suitcases?

My back and neck were aching. Here I was still bending over a pile of my belongings on the bare floor and could barely move a muscle to pack.

Imma insisted we check our luggage tonight at the Hillel Street depot, so we could take a morning bus to the airport and save money. But I was waiting and waiting for a miracle to keep us here. It was my last desperate hope. Only something miraculous would stop Imma from taking the flight from the Lod airport tomorrow. She's determined to go and won't listen to me. I wanted so hard to believe that Sarah's gift, *The Magician's Kit and Book of Enchantments*, would give me the power to change Imma's mind. It didn't work. Sarah's note made me cry:"...so whenever you feel lonesome, just say aloud the magic command and, in a jiffy, your genie will fly you back to us here."

I kissed her for the thought. But I needed to cast spells here and now over Imma to keep me in Yerushalayim.

I looked toward the window. No more would I see the lovely view of the Old City of Jerusalem from our fourth story apartment or the morning sun rising in the east, spreading its rays and chasing away the early shadows shrouding the white stone homes on the hillsides of my city, the view that gave me such an uplift in the early hours.

Now, it was dark outside. Was this really my last night in Jerusalem? I could not believe it. No more would I see my friends again or join them in our games and marches and celebrations. All my good times were over.

I was shaken. But what could I do? I was helpless. I turned back to fill up my suitcase.

My eyes wandered about the empty living room and to the balcony outside, now almost bare. How different it had looked, full of greenery, just a week ago. I took care of the garden where we kept our potted ferns and flowers. There I did my experiments with fruit and vegetable seeds planted in earth inside wooden boxes I had hammered together. Imma had bought me a shining brass sprinkling can for watering. And now I had to give my plants away – after all my tender loving care. I was going to miss them badly – and I know they're going to miss me.

One plant I could not give away: our grape vine, with its tendrils wrapped about the black iron railing. It grew from a cutting I planted four years ago in a large chipped clay pot I found. How surprised I was when it took root. I pruned the vine to keep it from growing wild or too large. We had enjoyed bunches of luscious grapes. Now, those renting our apartment will enjoy them. I don't mind but I hope they don't cut it down. I didn't have the heart to do it. It's a living thing.

One time during the year all our plants, except the vine, came indoors: right before Succot, to make room for building our succah.

"Your succah up there looks like a bright little home floating in the sky," Dvorah had said, as we were walking home from a holiday party.

"The light shining through the blue curtains makes it so different, up there by itself on your balcony, as if nothing keeps it attached to the earth, like a UFO from another planet."

I looked up. "It does look unusual. But it's so small. You're lucky your apartment is on the ground level so you can build a succah where our whole class can get together."

"But you have lots of visitors every day."

"We always have guests – to be more like a family, you know."

Yes, we did invite friends and neighbors into our succah to make up a family during this joyous season. I missed my father. Imma wouldn't invite him. My friends helped build and decorate each other's succahs by putting up drawings and posters, attaching colored streamers, hanging real carrots, apples, peppers, grapes, and birds made of egg-shells, as well as plastic and paper fruits and vegetables.

"Shoshi, please, don't dilly-dally and stop day-dreaming. We've got to finish tonight and take our luggage to the El Al office. You know we must leave very early tomorrow morning."

Well, I guess we're really going. There's nothing to stop Imma.

My mother usually spoke warmly and softly. This time her voice was screechy, high-pitched, tense and abrupt. Guess she must be exhausted.

How could I leave so quickly with no time for real good-byes to my friends?

"You had your party. How much more time do you want?" Imma shouted.

How did she read my thoughts?

The party was over... fading away. I felt so lonely again. I yearned so much. I had struggled and prayed hard against going away... and lost. Guess I must get on with my future.

With a burst of energy, I went through the pile on the floor and emptied box after box, stuffing all my clothing and precious things into the suitcase.

Completing the job was difficult, even though Imma had given me this piece of luggage just for my own personal things. It was so hard to choose. How could I leave most of my books and toys and everything? I squeezed in all I could and made sure nothing stuck out. The suitcase was full to bursting. I had to sit on it before I barely pulled the zippers together and locked them tight. Finally, I attached a label with our names: Shoshanna Bernstein, Mrs. Tova Bernstein, and our temporary Harvard address.

"Shoshi, are you done? I need some help here."

"I'm coming, Imma."

I was happy Imma had called me. I must keep busy doing things to forget.

Imma opened the door to our apartment and pressed the button for the stairway light. I helped her drag the boxes and luggage down three flights of stairs. We stood in the darkened, cool, open hallway, all worn out, and hoping the cab would arrive quickly.

II
FLIGHT OVERSEAS

I was sleepy the next morning when Imma woke me up and rushed us to the Lod airport so we would arrive in time to make our overseas flight. . As I settled in my window seat, I tried to recall my distressing dream from last night, but the picture was already fading, of tossing seas, of pounding storms outside....

I peered through the small glass oval at my side. Pitch darkness there, seen through a foggy pane. As if nothing was outside. Only the people in this "ark" would rise above the flood and be saved.

Where were the animals? In another part of this vast ship? I hope the pilot (was he Noah?) took along plenty of food for the journey. After all, they cannot wait until a dove brings an olive branch.

Tears welled up in my eyes. How I loved to feed Shirah, my beautiful yellow canary, who sang only for me. She was my first pet. I had picked out the bird stand and cage and put them in a corner of my bedroom. I would wake up and lie down to warbling music. Mother said I had to give her away. I could not bring her to America.

Dvorah could not adopt Shirah – and it made me sad. Her mother was allergic to bird feathers. So I gave my bird to Ednah, who loved pets, along with all the food boxes and care instructions. Ednah promised to write and tell me how Shirah was getting along and not to let any four-legged pets near her.

Well – maybe, just maybe – Imma would let me get another canary. It would still not be the same.

"Dear, here's a lemon drop for you to suck on when the plane starts. It's supposed to help with the pressure you feel in your ears. This is really your first long-distance plane ride."

"You know I love hard candy. I'll take it. Imma, when are we starting? We've been sitting here doing nothing."

"Sooner than you think. See those lit-up signs: 'Fasten seatbelts.'"

I clicked on my seatbelt and gazed out to take my last view of Israel.

The haze was fading and light was spreading. What I saw was not pleasant.

All about were enormous planes standing, landing, or taking off. Workers were filling open trucks attached to small jeeps with all kinds of objects removed from the belly of large airplanes. I was too far away to see exactly but I thought it must be the luggage. Some men in tank cars were speeding to planes and attaching pipelines while others were clambering all over the planes like busy monkeys. I suppose they were just making sure the ride would be safe.

I felt the plane slowly turning. Powerful motors were whirring. The plane was picking up speed, roaring straight ahead. The sounds were speaking to me, trying to tell me about the future. Suddenly I became thrilled all over, from my head to my toes. Something was happening to me. Great events must be coming. Within seconds the aircraft reached the edge of the tarmac, snapped its bonds to earth, and streaked into the sky.

Soon my ears felt clogged and pounded within. I sucked hard on the candy. I peered out again. We were in the midst of a dense fog but it did not last. In a few moments the plane rose again. Alongside the plane I saw a layer of soft, fluffy clouds like enormous cotton balls.

Before long they too disappeared. On the ground below appeared a child's complete village: streets lined with houses, trees, and lights, wide roads filled with traveling cars, trucks, and buses, and small dots – were they people? – entering and leaving different buildings. As I was enjoying this sight, it began to fade, getting smaller and smaller until all I could see were lines, thin lines of wide highways, rivers, city outlines, and finally just a sea coast. My past life was vanishing fast.

A new world was expanding before me. Above, a glorious sun

was shining in the bluest sky. Below was the open sea as wide and as far as I could see. It was all so wonderful, so different, like another beginning after the flood. Yes, that must be the sign. My eyes and ears were now clear. I would start a new life for myself, yet not forget the old.

"Would you like your breakfast?"

The stewardess's words startled me. I looked up into her eyes, then at the large wheeled cart laden with numerous trays containing food. Many passengers, I noticed, were already eating. I nodded.

The stewardess lowered the table leaf and put down the breakfast tray.

I relished the cool, wet, fresh taste of the orange juice. I sipped it slowly. Only as I began to chew did I realize how hungry I was. I just had a small bun and glass of milk that morning before leaving the apartment.

I felt free, refreshed and restless. I raised myself up and strained my neck. The plane was full: mostly grown-ups, lots of children, including babies, a few whimpering as they slept. I thought that later I would take a walk around the plane.

Imma was holding an open paperback novel in her hands. She was staring ahead rather than reading it. Was she thinking about what she left behind too?

"Imma," I said, gently touching her wrist, "you know this is the first time in a long while we've sat together so quietly and didn't have to rush about doing things."

Imma, smiling, turned to me.

"You're right. We're always busy – every day of the week. I have to go to the University to teach classes, do my writing and research and then come home to run the apartment. Often, when I'd rather be with you, I prepare work and do writing at home, too."

"And I have to go to school and do homework. I really don't have that much time to be with my friends. You know I do help you in lots of ways. Then, I'm involved with all my special activities – drama club and science club. Even on Shabbat we have to prepare and serve our invited guests and then I run off to my afternoon Bnei Akiva group."

"It's no wonder we get worn out and cross with each other."

"I love you, Imma." I burst out and put my arm about her.

"I know you do – and I love you."

"I do miss Abba and the three of us being together. Now we rarely see him." I saw the muscles in Imma's face tighten.

"Yes, it's true. It doesn't make me happy."

"He said he'd help us pack, and meet us at the airport."

"That's Abba. He told me he might go to Haifa. He'll probably write you a letter and explain.

"You know, Imma, I can always depend on you, but Abba always disappoints me. I never know what to expect."

"He's not a bad person – just forgetful and negligent. He thinks too much about himself and what he wants and doesn't think enough about others. He enjoyed playing with you when you were younger.

"Remember when he got down on the floor like a pony to give you a ride on his back as we played the record, 'Riding piggy-back with Daddy.' And the time he took you to a kibbutz in the Galil to help gather in the produce. And when you were both at a dig working so carefully on the ground with small tools and brushes to find artifacts."

"That was great. And I found a small oil lamp all by myself."

"He was so proud of you – and went all over showing it off."

Suddenly I glanced up at Imma. She was smiling pleasantly, but her eyes were glistening.

"Do you still love him?" I saw Imma turn red and faltered.

"In some ways... in my memories... not as a real person. People often change in time. We were separated over three years ago....

"He changed first. You know he wanted the divorce. He wanted to be free – to come and go as he wished."

"Yes, I know, Imma. He broke up the family. That was when I really hated him – and I wrote and told him. But I was thinking hard about it, about all that happened. Was it all his fault? Maybe, just maybe something you did made him want to go away?"

"What do you mean – something I did?" Imma looked like she was ready to boil, her eyes were flashing.

"Why are you getting mad at me? I was just wondering... maybe something you did bothered him... I don't know... the way you said something... and he couldn't take it? I saw you get angry at him."

"No, I didn't... well, he did make me angry at times and I screamed at him once or twice, like when he quit his job over something very small. Or, when he was supposed to buy something for the house and instead brought home a bunch of architecture books under his arm."

"Was that all?"

"What do you mean – all? He just used money for what he wanted and went wherever he wanted to go – often without us. Isn't that why I had to find a part-time job so we could live? It just made me more and more furious."

"Maybe he could not take it, the way you spoke to him?"

"He forced me to act that way. He started it. I was always willing to try to get along but he was not. It was his way or nothing."

"Mother, I'm so sorry."

"There's much more we could discuss but maybe we should wait and talk about it later. It's more important right now to plan ahead for our new life at Harvard."

"You're right, Imma. And we do have each other."

I kissed her on the cheek and squeezed her hand.

"I think, Imma, I'll take a rest just now. I have so much to think over."

I felt calm and relaxed, and soon my eyes closed gently.

Suddenly I heard the pilot's voice booming over the loudspeaker.

"Ladies and gentlemen, please fasten your seatbelts. We have run into some minor turbulence."

In a moment the plane seemed to be picked up by invisible giant hands and tossed about. I heard food trays smashing to the floor. Some parcels and clothing from the bins overhead scattered into the air. I felt myself lifted up and thrust down like I was in an elevator gone berserk. I was terrified. We were going to crash!

"Imma, I'm scared. Something terrible is happening. The airplane is going to break up. I know it will."

"No, dear. Try to stay calm. We ran into some strong winds, that's all."

"No, we're in danger. Let's go back, let's go back to Israel. This is a bad sign. It means we shouldn't have come."

"We can't go back and we're not going back," Imma said sternly. "Take hold of yourself. We've got bigger problems than this ahead."

Frightened by her words, I glanced up at Imma. Then I leaned back on the seat and shut my eyes tight. I did not want to see anything any more.

III
SEARCHING FOR A HOME

I was having the greatest adventure of my life, excited and confused at the same time. A lot was happening fast. Within twenty-four hours – just one full day – I had traveled by bus from Jerusalem to Lod, flown with El Al to Heathrow airport at London, then to the Kennedy airport in New York City, finally to land at the Logan airport in Boston. We would soon be on our way to Harvard University's Faculty Club where Imma had arranged to stay the next few days while looking for a suitable year-long apartment.

We had a short wait in the New York airport baggage room to pick up our things. All the passengers rushed to load their luggage on carts and move into lines. It didn't do any good though because the lines were so slow. I became impatient.

"Imma," I asked, "why are they so slow? Why are we wasting time?"

"Shoshi, these are customs lines. Everyone from overseas has to go through them. It takes time. First, you have to show your passport with your picture so they know who you are. Then, you may need to show the contents of your luggage. There are laws as to what and how much you can bring in. The officers have to check for forbidden items and the allowed amounts of other items like liquor. Sometimes United States citizens are not bothered too much and go through without too much questioning."

"But, Imma, I thought you were an Israeli."

"I am. We came on aliyah when we were married. But America and Israel allow you to have dual citizenship. That means we could choose to be citizens of both countries – and we did. I would not want to give up my American citizenship. It's too precious."

"Am I an American citizen, Imma?"

"Yes, you are. When you were born we went to the American consul – he's the person who takes care of American interests in Israel – and registered your birth. That made you an American citizen. So, although you have never been in America before, you can still feel at home."

I smiled and looked into Imma's eyes.

"I knew I could depend on you. You're always taking good care of me."

The custom officers were busy. When Imma showed them her papers and Harvard position they let us through without delay.

"We were lucky, Imma. This was a good day to come."

"I guess so. After all, what could two simple women do," she laughed, and I laughed with her.

"It's because of these customs officers that I couldn't bring my canary, right?" We both laughed again.

It was a short trip to Boston by plane. The taxi ride to Harvard and the Faculty Club seemed longer.

"We can't afford to pay for rides like these," Imma said. "We'll have to learn to use the city buses and trains, since we have no car. I heard that the train system here is excellent."

"I don't mind. It will be more fun getting around that way."

Through the taxi's windows I enjoyed watching the scenery by the Charles River as we went along Memorial Drive. Soon Harvard University was in front of us. Traffic congestion slowed us down so we had time to look around.

"Imma, I recognize some of those old brick buildings. They look like a picture you showed me of Independence Hall and old houses in Philadelphia where the United States began. They have the same long chimneys sticking out of their roofs. No houses in Israel have them. I guess because it's warmer there. Other buildings remind me of the Greek temples in Abba's books on architecture, with their tall white pillars.

"They don't look half as beautiful as the new stone buildings of the Hebrew University that seem to grow out of the side of Mount Scopus. It's a lot more natural there, with grass, trees and flowers."

"I feel the same way, Shoshi. You have to remember, though, Harvard is almost 350 years old and the Hebrew University is only about sixty years old. So it would have to be newer and different.

"Shoshi, look at the traffic. We're hardly moving. Reminds me of the narrow streets of Yerushalayim. I'm glad we don't have a car. There would be no place to park it."

"And look at all the people," I added. "It's so crowded. I suppose most of them are students and professors here. I guess Harvard is larger than the Hebrew University, but it's not as nice."

I liked the registrar at the Faculty Club. He had the key to our room ready when we arrived and helped us take up our luggage. There was a note for us at the desk.

Though tired, we put our things away. I felt exhausted and, still dressed, I flopped into bed, unable to keep my eyes open. Suddenly, a fire engine siren clanged away. I tried to ignore the loud blasting sound, but I lost the battle. It awakened me. Half-opening my eyes, I could see Imma put down the telephone.

"Somebody called us? Who was it?"

"Dr. Weatherall, my boss, who left the note. He's head of the

Department of Social Sciences and wanted to be sure to welcome me as soon as I arrived. He sends regards to you, too. He wants to be of help."

"Imma, why am I so sleepy? I feel like I could close my eyes and forget everything for a week."

"It's no wonder. Outside it's afternoon, but it's 3 am for your body and mine. They call that 'jet lag.' Count your travel hours. Let's take a shower and go right to bed. We have a big day tomorrow. We need to find a permanent home.

"While you were napping, I called the Harvard Housing Office rental agents and some people our friends in Israel recommended who might have apartments to rent. We'll start fresh and early. Lucky we have about a week before you start Rambam school."

The next morning at the Housing Office, Imma spoke to the clerk.

"I'm here on a one-year instructorship and require housing for myself and my daughter. You have my application."

"Yes, after you called we checked your file. We received your application, and, while we have available apartments, we regret that our rental fees might be too high for you to handle."

"But I'm employed by the University."

"We are sorry. Rental charges are set alike for all faculty members."

"Thank you, but where do I turn now?

"To the walls behind you, where the students are copying down addresses from the posts on the wall. There are numerous, fine private rental apartments listed in all the surrounding townships."

Imma surveyed the many listings and found a few in Cambridge, Newton, and Brookline worth copying. I helped to write some of them down on cards.

"Shoshi, we're going to look around before making up our minds. You see, apartments are very expensive here, more than in

Israel. You heard the clerk say I was probably not earning enough to be able to pay for University apartments.

"In a way, I'm happy it worked out this way. I prefer to find a place in Brookline, which is next to Boston. Living in Cambridge would be fine for me, but you wouldn't have any friends or classmates or school nearby or any synagogue with young people your age. And I don't know about the shopping.

"I think we need two bedrooms. Then you'll l be able to invite your friends to stay overnight and I won't bother you if I stay up late writing in the evenings.

"Though it costs more, I think we'll get a furnished apartment. I don't think we have the time or patience to go around finding and buying or renting furniture and other items."

"Thanks, Imma, you're great." I took my mother's hand and held it fast.

It was late afternoon when we got back to the Faculty Club, exhausted but undecided. The rental agents had driven us to many apartments and homes. Some were beautiful with plants or grounds but were very expensive. Those we could afford were in poor condition. Most were located far from train lines. It would take too long to walk to the stations.

"Tomorrow we will go by ourselves, only to Brookline. We have maps and can learn where the other students live by checking the class lists the Rambam School sent us. We have addresses, including those from our Israeli friends, and can meet the owners there," said Imma.

At the end of the second day of searching, we were dragging our legs from exhaustion, but happier. That evening we sat down, discussed our choices and agreed. We'd take a two-bedroom suite in a newly renovated apartment building. It would cost a little more but all the rooms were freshly painted, the furnishings clean and in good condition and the kitchen equipped with new appliances ("so they don't have to be kashered"). The view from our second-floor windows took in the trees and flowers on the building grounds and a grassy play field across the street. And we both had one pleasant surprise: There was a desk with a lamp in each bedroom.

"It's almost perfect," said Imma joyfully. "I'll still have to take the train to Harvard and we'll have to arrange school transportation for you. But you'll have classmates nearby, a library where I know you'll keep busy, stores for shopping, and a synagogue where you'll make new friends."

"Imma, you're just wonderful. I feel a lot better now."

"Well, we're not moving in for a couple of days and our problems aren't over. You're next in line. Tomorrow, we go to your school."

"But, Imma," I blurted out, "I'm afraid – starting off in a new school and a new country."

"Why, Shoshi, we're in America – and you know English very well. Even though you spoke Hebrew everywhere, including school, we always spoke English at home and I had you read all those English books – fairy tales, histories, and books on science you liked. It should be very easy for you."

"It's not the same thing."

"Of course not, but you won't have any problems."

"But I lost all my school friends, I feel all alone."

"You didn't lose them – and, besides, as I said before, you'll soon have new ones. There's nothing to worry about."

But I was still worrying... about a lot of things.

IV
A New School

Imma was bent over, weeping with all her heart. Her palms were gripping the sides of her head and her fingertips were digging into her hair. "How can I make it? How are we going to live?" she was crying in despair.

I became agitated and feverish. Was Imma counting cash, putting money into different piles to pay for bills she owed? Her checkbook was lying open in front of her unused. The rest of the table was bare.

It's because of me; it's my fault. She's spending all her money to make me happy. Why did I make her do it?

I jumped up in bed, startled and distressed. I stared straight ahead. There was Imma at the table, holding the phone to her ear with one hand and jotting notes on slips of paper with the other.

"What is it, Soshi? You look scared."

"Oh, Imma. I was worried about you." I was afraid to tell her about the money.

"I'm making calls to learn about trains from here to Rambam school. Let's hurry so we can make the most of today."

We had to take two trains. One track traveled from Cambridge to Boston and the other back to Brookline. On the trip I found time to ask Imma the questions I'd been bursting with.

"Imma, I feel so bad. I'm making you pay so much for the apartment... and you told me school costs a lot, too. How will you manage? Abba is not sending you any money."

Imma smiled, as always, and put her arm about me.

"Thank you for being so concerned. Yes, school does cost money because Rambam is a private school and Evelina de Rothshild was a public school in Israel. The Rambam program fits best the kind of studies you had there. I know you'll like it. Besides, they may not charge me as much because of my low income. If things get bad, I have some savings we could use."

"You know, Imma, I didn't want to come. So don't blame me. You made me come and I don't know why. We were happy in Israel." I was getting angry.

"I thought I explained it to you. Harvard is the oldest university in America; it's an honor to be asked to teach here. And since you talk about wanting to be a psychologist, a hundred years ago, here at Harvard, Dr. William James wrote *Principles of Psychology*, the first book on this subject in the United States."

"Who cares about all that?! It's NOT the reason you came," I interrupted –I must have been screaming – "Why did they have to pick on you?"

"Because everyone – well, not everyone – is concerned with the Holocaust."

"Yes, yes, I know all about it," I answered, calming down. "Our teachers discussed it and showed us movies. Some of my classmates' parents were saved. But you didn't answer my question. Why did they pick on YOU?" I was raising my voice again.

"Remember," Imma said so softly, "I was working part-time at the University doing research, talking to many people who came out of the Holocaust and to their children. Then I was busy writing papers about what I had learned. After the divorce they asked me to continue my work and teach full-time. I guess Harvard – or maybe just Dr. Weatherall – heard or read about my studies. No one was here in this field, and I think maybe they wanted a woman. So I was picked. Besides, I felt strongly that more students, future teachers, should understand how the Holocaust affected people, especially Jews, and their children and future generations."

"Thanks for telling me, Imma. I still don't want to be here, but now I know you didn't come just to make money."

"I also came to learn as well as to teach."

I turned serious and stopped talking. Imma noticed but said nothing.

"We're almost there. At the next stop we get off the T Train and we'll be a short distance from the school."

We crossed over, walked up the street and came face-to-face with a tall brick wall surrounding buildings with rounded red tile roofs. We climbed up a circular path on a hilly street and entered the school grounds.

Inside only a few students were around. They must be new students, too, I thought. The grown-ups were probably teachers. I felt strange, as if I did not belong there. It was all so new.

"Imma, you talk to them, please. I'm afraid." I gripped my mother's hand.

"Good morning," Imma said, approaching one of the men. "I'm looking for Rabbi Weiner and Dr. Rosenberg, who want to see my daughter."

"Mrs. Bernstein, we've been expecting you. I'm Dr. Rosenberg. This is your daughter, Shoshanna? Good morning, Shoshanna. We're happy to have you with us."

"I'm glad to be here," I said politely, but I didn't mean it.

"If you don't mind, we'd like to see what levels you are up to, so we'll know where you'll fit best. Is that all right?"

"Yes, I guess," I replied, still scared. I didn't expect to take any tests.

Dr. Rosenberg took me by the hand as we walked down the corridor to a vacant classroom.

Imma waited. In less than an hour I was back with Dr. Rosenberg.

"Mrs. Bernstein, I have excellent news. Shoshanna surprised us. Not only in Hebrew where we thought she would excel, but also in English. She reads quite well and with understanding. We were impressed with her English speech and the lack of any speech accent."

"You know, she was born in Israel, but we spoke English at home and provided her with books suitable for her age level. She has an acute ear for sound and sings well, too."

"Oh, Imma. You didn't have to tell him that," I said, embarrassed.

"I'm sure she does," Dr. Rosenberg said. "As I told Shoshanna, we plan to place her in the Honors program in Hebrew and science and give her a full secular program in all areas. We learned she enjoys experiments and knows a good deal about botany.

"Moreover," he continued, "we're hoping Shoshanna will help us. As you may realize, one of our goals is to interest our students in, and get them excited about Israel. Since Shoshanna has lived all her life there and speaks English so well, she's the ideal person to inspire our students by telling them about her experiences there – in brief, to make the Land of Israel beautiful, vital, and real. I can see how much she misses her homeland."

I looked up at Imma, not knowing what to say.

"Thank you," Imma replied, "I hope my daughter can live up to your many expectations."

After touring the school, filling out school records and getting a set of classroom forms, we were on our way back to Harvard.

"Imma," I complained as we were riding on the T Train, "I'm still scared."

"What about now?" Imma said, annoyed. "You see the school is beautiful – the library, the science labs, the classrooms, the grounds – everything."

"Yes, I know, but they are expecting too much. You saw the schedule. A long day, with so many classes, and an honors program, too. And I don't know what my classmates are like. I don't know if they'll like me."

"Of course they will." Imma put her arm about me. "Let's talk about something pleasant. I must go to my department office to straighten out some things. Then I'll take you to see something unusual. Nearby is the Botanical Museum where they have over 700 different kinds of flowers, all true-to-life, in glass."

"I'd rather see real flowers," I said, scowling.

"Why must you criticize everything instead of enjoying what you have?"

Later, on our way back to the Faculty Club, I felt apologetic.

"Imma, I want you to know I appreciate all you're doing. It doesn't mean I have to like everything. I did enjoy the Glass Museum and the other museums we looked at and the Heritage Tour you took me on. I learned a lot. Now, I'm tired enough to flop right into bed."

Within our room I fell down into bed, totally exhausted. Imma had to make more calls, she said, "to arrange for your transportation to school, Shoshi. I'm tired, too."

"Imma, I wish you wouldn't say that. You make me feel guilty. I didn't ask to come here and give you all this trouble."

"I'm sorry. You're right. I'll try to watch myself."

She telephoned parents on my list asking whether they had any place in their car pool for one more student.

"You see," she would try to explain, "I have no car, so I can't offer my turn. We just came from Israel. I would be glad to help in other ways."

The answers were: "Sorry, we have a full car;" "If you can't help us, we can't help you;" and "We'll see; we'll get back to you."

"Shoshi, I'm having trouble finding a car pool. We may have to walk. There is no direct bus or train from our apartment in Brookline to the school and I can't afford to pay for a taxi every day."

By the time she was finished with her calls, I was fast asleep.

In the morning, a ringing of the phone jarred me awake.

"Mrs. Bernstein?"

"Yes."

"This is Mrs. Sanders, a parent of one of the girls in your daughter's class at Rambam. I just found out she's a new student in the class and I didn't want to exclude her from my daughter's bat mitzvah, which will take place this coming Sunday. Please tell her she's welcome and we're all looking forward to meeting her."

"Thank you very much. We both appreciate your calling and invitation."

"Shoshi, wake up," Imma shouted. She really shook me up.

"What happened? You found a car pool?" "It's bad news and good news."

"What is it, please?"

"So far, nobody wants to help with transportation. Some people are too selfish to help a stranger. Others welcome you before you ask. That's the great news. You were just invited to the bat mitzvah of one of the girls in your new class. Wasn't that a thoughtful thing to do? You'll meet the members of your class there and some faculty members."

"Thanks. For that I don't mind you're waking me up. Now, I can sleep in peace, I hope."

"This is your last night to sleep here. Enjoy it. Tomorrow we move to our new apartment."

V
MEETING OLD FRIENDS

I thought I was dreaming. I thought I heard the outside bell ringing. The haulers were there. They picked up box after box, package after package, all the luggage. Together they managed to carry the trunk down the three flights of stairs. Soon their truck took off to our new home and Imma and I followed.

That was the way it had always been. Every one or two years, another apartment change. From third floor to second floor to fourth floor... from street to street, from Jabotinsky to Palmach, from Palmach to Ibn Ezra, from Ibn Ezra to Balfour. Always on the go, moving again and again. No home to call our own. No room or corner to call mine.

"Now, it's different," Imma said. "This is our own place. We scrimped and saved and bought our own apartment. You have your own room. Nobody can touch it or tell you what to bring into it or what to hang up. But you'll have to keep it clean," Imma smiled.

"What's all that noise at the walls, Imma?"

"The men are putting up shelves for your books and

mine. We need them right away."

Finally, after years of waiting, it really happened. I can't believe it. We have a home all our own.

The pounding started again, this time on the floor. I jumped up. Imma was packing suitcases. I was in a daze.

"Imma, What are you doing? We don't have to move any more. We can stay here."

"Shoshi, what ARE you talking about? Wake up. We're in a hurry. I've ordered a cab to be here in an hour. Get ready."

It was the same as before; nothing's changed. It was only a dream. For a while I had felt so great.

From the cab's windows we could see the complex ahead with its garden patio. The apartment was still beautiful and I loved the view from my bedroom window. I stood there taking it all in.

"Later, Shoshi. First take care of your things, especially your good blue dress for the bat mitzvah. They left hangers in the closets."

Imma was happy the gas and electricity had been turned on and the telephone was working. Our next job was to check the stores in the neighborhood.

"Well," I said on the way back from our tour, "we found a butcher and baker but no candlestick maker. We don't need him."

"We also saw the library again and the Purity Supreme Supermarket where we're going as soon as I buy a shopping cart to take food home."

"Imma, I saw some in front of a hardware store across the street. I'm all set with my school supplies – I hope – and letter sheets and stamps so I can start writing letters."

"Not yet. It's Friday and we must get ready for Shabbat. I want to take a walk to your school to see how long it takes, in case you have no ride for Tuesday when school begins."

The one-way walk to Rambam took about forty minutes.

After getting the cart on our return, we began our food buying. "Shoshi," a voice screamed over the heads of the shoppers.

I recognized the voice and screeched. I turned around and ran towards the voice as a girl my age was running towards me. We hugged and squeezed each other.

"What are you doing here?" we both exploded at the same time. My friend was faster to answer.

"You know I was only in Israel for one year. I live here. You forgot."

"We're in Boston for only one year – at least, that's what my mother says."

"Where are you staying?"

"In the Clifford Complex."

"We live only four blocks away!! Why don't you have Shabbat lunch with us?"

"I'd love to, Adele. I'll ask Imma."

I didn't have to. Imma was right there. She had recognized the voice, too.

"Adele, how are you? It feels so good to find somebody we know. How's your family? How are your parents?"?"

"They're OK. Would you, please, come to us for Shabbat lunch?"

Imma smiled. "We'd be delighted to come. Does your mother know about it?"

"I'll get her right away." In a moment her mother appeared, dragging her cart behind her with Adele pulling at her sleeve. Imma held her arms out.

"Batyah, what a wonderful surprise! You have no idea what it means to find a familiar face," my mother said.

Our mothers embraced warmly.

"Shoshi, welcome to Boston. Adele's offer is always good. We'll expect you at lunch tomorrow. Wait. Where shall we meet? We usually go to the Brookline Synagogue on Pleasant Street. Do you know where it is? Can you get there?"

"Isn't that a coincidence? That's where we had planned to go. I'm used to following maps. We'll meet you there."

"You'll like Rabbi and Rebbetzin Freiberg. Everybody does. It's a warm congregation with lots of young people."

VI
LEARNING ABOUT MY PAST

We spent the rest of the afternoon cleaning and preparing for Shabbat. I was in charge of setting the table. On a clean tablecloth I centered our two candlesticks. In front of them I put a bottle of wine, the *kiddush* cups and the silver tray, with its two challahs and knife covered with a Shabbat cloth. I liked the European style of placing the silverware on three sides of the plates. I learned that when I was a guest in Daniela's Viennese parental home in Yerushalayim.

As usual, we said our evening prayers at home. Imma made the blessing over the candles ushering in the Shabbat queen. We took turns saying the *kiddush* over wine, sanctifying the Shabbat.

After slicing the challah, while we were eating, I looked up at Imma.

"Imma, would this be a good time to talk?"

"Of course. Why do you ask?"

"Because there are things about your life you never told me. I was afraid to ask before. Now I must ask. I'm bursting."

"Go ahead, if you must. I hope it doesn't spoil our meal."

"I hope not. If it does, we can stop. I wouldn't want it to ruin our

Shabbat – but it's about that, too.

"We're all alone. We've been alone for a long time. We used to sing – the three of us – every Shabbat eve and afternoon. We loved our Shabbat meals together. Now, there's no man in the house to make *kiddush* or *havdalah* or anything. I know we do it, but it's not the same."

"Shoshi, you know I can't change that. I didn't want it this way."

"Then why did it have to happen?"

"We went over all that before. For your sake, I'll repeat it. Let's make this the last time, because it bothers me deeply. Abba is a very intelligent person, an excellent architect. He might have been an excellent father, too. He was for a while. His problem is he likes to do things his own way and is not aware of other people's needs.

"You've heard of Peter Pan. I think you saw the play. That's your father. He always wants to be young, flitting about, doing what he pleases, living in fantasy. Peter Pan wasn't a bad person. He never grew up, never took responsibility."

I laughed. "I remember the story. He was a grown-up child. But he was so adorable, lively and jolly, full of fun and adventure – and so believable."

"Yes, up to a point. In the end others got tired of his playfulness."

"I guess you're right. That was only my first question, my first step. The next question is tougher." I tried to smile.

"Can it wait until I get the soup?"

"Of course, Imma. Is it the *gruenkern* soup? I love it."

"Yes."

When I finished the last drop of the luscious soup, I was warmed up.

"OK, let's forget about Abba. Where's the rest of the family? We don't have anybody. No grandparents, no aunts or uncles, no cousins, nobody. The thing is that I don't even know very much about my own family. It's not fair. Everybody needs a family. Imma, you're great, but two persons are not enough to make a family, a real living, happy family. Sometimes, I feel desperate."

Slowly Imma finished chewing the piece of roast chicken in her mouth.

"You're right, but there's nothing I can do about that either. I could tell you more to make you feel better – I hope."

"Great. Let's get started. There is a lot I want to learn. First, about the Holocaust. How does our family fit in? Did anybody reach Eretz Yisrael?"

"No one reached "Israel"; no Medinat Yisrael existed then. Some tried to reach the land, called Palestine in those days, and got caught. Remember the story of Hannah Szenes and how she tried to save Jews by smuggling them to Israel? You know what happened to her."

"Were they all killed? Is that why you didn't want to say anything to me?"

"In part. It's going to be a long family tree lesson. Can you take it?"

"Sure. I'm ready."

"Let's begin with Abba. His parents came to America when they were young and have since died. He has an older brother somewhere in the States. We lost touch with him before we left for Israel. The rest of his family lived in Russia. Most of them, as far as we know, were caught by the Nazis when they invaded Russia. Two of his cousins died in the war fighting for the U.S.S.R. They're probably all gone now.

"My family came from Germany. My own grandparents would not budge. 'It will all blow over,' they said. They were well off and wanted to keep it all. "How wrong they were. My own parents did not believe that. They were married before the war began. By the time I was two, it was getting harder to get out. My uncle and aunt, my mother's sister, left for America and took me with them. My mother, your Savta, could not leave Saba, who was ill. My aunt and uncle raised me, but they never let me forget my parents. I learned that my parents were taken by the Nazis to a concentration camp where Saba soon died."

"So you never saw your own parents since you were two years old?"

"Yes."

"What happened to Savta?" I asked.

"We're not sure. Letters were exchanged for a while. My aunt and uncle moved from Springfield, Ohio, to Chicago and soon after no more mail arrived.

"That's when we think she was taken to a concentration camp. By the time I was married my aunt and uncle had died. We never found out what happened to Savta, although we tried hard to locate her.

"Yes, I haven't been with my mother since I was two years old.

"You have been more fortunate."

"Imma, I feel so sorry for you."

"You're the last of our long family line. Let me show you something."

Imma brought over her wallet and took out a picture she carried with her.

"Shoshi, here's the only picture I have with me of my early childhood."

With trembling hands, I took it from her. I saw a picture of a round-cheeked baby, with a head full of curls, dressed in a long white lace gown staring upward with a puzzled expression on her face.

"Imma, this is beautiful. It must be your baby picture. You were very pretty then too. I don't recall seeing it."

"Yes, you did, when you were much younger. I also showed you other things. Think hard. Do you remember the black, lacquered box with the little red velvet ring box and the red velvet case inside?"

"I think I do... Was there a baby ring with two letters on it? I don't remember clearly what they were."

"Yes, a baby ring with the initials: T. K."

"What was your name then?"

"Tova Kornblatt. I let you open the ring box and the velvet case. Do you remember what was in the case?"

"Now I can see it in my mind. Old letters and a locket with two pictures."

"You do remember! The locket has pictures of my parents, and the letters in German, are from my mother. I put them all in our safe deposit box at the bank. The locket and ring are very precious and I don't want to lose them. The letters are very old and delicate. I was afraid they might be harmed."

"What were your parents' names?"

"Serena, for Sarah, Kornblatt and Max, for Moshe, Kornblatt."

"At least, now I know their names – for the first time."

"I rarely looked at the locket with my parents' pictures or the ring. After the divorce, when I felt alone, I took them out and kept them close to me for a long while. I needed them and cried over them many times."

"Oh, Imma."

"All right, let's talk a little more. You think you're lonesome. What about me?Now, I have only you. You have parents, lots of friends and can make more. Sure, I knew a few mothers of your classmates in Israel and professors at the Hebrew University, but that was all.

"I could not talk to them like you talk to your friends. Abba deserted us. I went to work and I have been too busy to find time to relax...."

We kept talking all Shabbat eve into the late hours of the night about our family and the Holocaust.

After that long time together, I tossed in bed that night. I was very troubled, wondering, *how can I help Imma?* She's so alone and has been through so much. And I wondered what happened to our family. Were they all really lost? I have so much to learn and to do.

> *There was a knock on the door in the early darkness of night. I was ready. My sharp ear had been tuned in while my body was sleeping all dressed on top of the spread. Trying to control my trembling I got out of bed, shoes in hand. I tip-toed to my parents' room. They were up. "We must wake up Saba Moshe and Saba Yohanan and Savta Sarah and Savta Leah."*
>
> *"Yes, of course," Abba whispered, "we must hurry."*
>
> *I had planned and timed all this before. We walked single-file to the kitchen, Abba first and Imma last. Abba moved aside a wall cabinet full of dishes and pots and pans and opened a secret sliding panel he had built.*
>
> *With his flashlight he led the way for them to pass through before he put everything back in place.*
>
> *It all took less than thirty seconds. The knock became a little louder. We had left the door unlocked and the beds made so the intruders, the murderers, would think we were out visiting or had already been taken. All they were after were human beings to destroy. As we went down the special steps to the hidden basement, we heard pounding on other doors, screaming and shouting, and shooting in the streets. I put my hands tightly over my ears to shut it all out.*

Abba had provided our hideout with all kinds of foods, even a toilet. Still, I wondered, how long could we hold out. I looked at my Sabas and Savtas. They were old, worn out by age, lack of sleep and rest, fear and loss of appetite. Would we be able to take care of them living this way? It bothered me. Yet, I was afraid to ask questions.

Abba bent down to the floor, removed the grating over the drain, lifted out a metal container and placed it on the table. He opened the lid and retrieved a notebook. For some time, by the dim light of a kerosene lamp, he wrote. Then he replaced the notebook and put everything back in place.

"Some day," he said, "researchers will find this place. Some day the world will know what happened here. Some day future Jewish generations will learn the true story of our family."

I listened, tried to understand, but was too weary. It was quiet now, a deathly silence. Soon my eyes were closed.

VII
MY MOTHER'S PROBLEM

I was in a daze when I opened my eyes that Shabbat morning. Sunlight was streaming in through the windows. Imma was just getting up too. We washed and dressed in a hurry, but still arrived at shul late. The Torah was already open on the central *bimah* and the reader was chanting the weekly portion. I strained to see Adele and her family but could not find them.

I wonder if Adele's family was up late last night arguing about her parents staying together. She once told me they were having problems. I hope it's not serious.

I sat down in the women's section next to Imma and took out an English Torah to find the chapter in Deuteronomy that was being read. That's funny, I thought. It's about Imma's problem. A man loves a woman and later does not want her.

Later I found Adele sitting several rows behind me. She must have entered by an upper stairway. We waved to each other. I felt relieved.

During the service, I started to carry out my promise to make sure Imma is not alone any more. I searched for a man not too young or too old, not married and not plain-looking, with or without a beard, tall enough for her to look up to and nicely dressed – someone Imma would like. I looked round and found three men I liked. When the service ended, I watched women approaching all three. I was so disappointed! All my hopes for nothing. I guess the best men are grabbed first.

Our two families got together as we left the synagogue. Dr. Tanarof led us on a walking tour on the way to his home. The only site I remember was the house where President John F. Kennedy was born. I had heard of him. At Adele's house Dr. Tanarof was bubbling with song and energy. When his two daughters set the table, we offered to help, but they said it wasn't necessary. As Mrs. Tanarof got the food ready, Dr. Tanarof discussed his pieces of sculpture and paintings. I especially liked the painting "Rebecca at the Well," with the little lamb looking up at his shepherdess.

I was overjoyed that for the first time in a long to hear a man saying the *kiddush*. I could see Abba standing there with cup in hand. I would join him for the *brachah* over bread, as he held the two challahs in his hands.

"Adele," I called across the table, "I guess we're going to be classmates again. You were in my class last year."

"I don't think so. I'm going to another school."

"Why? We could see each other and go to school together and have fun."

"I went to Rambam the year before last. The kids are very clicky and snooty and stick together. It's hard to break in. Besides, they give you a lot of homework. I won't have time to enjoy myself."

My jaw dropped. I glanced at Imma. I did not know what to say at first. Then I smiled.

"School starts Tuesday. I'll see what it's like. I can always change my mind."

Imma stared at me but said nothing.

We sang *zemirot* throughout the meal. I joined in loudly and felt great. I didn't care what Imma thought. I wanted to be with Adele, my long-time friend.

" Batyah, we enjoyed your culinary talents and, Dave, thank you for your entertainment. We want you all to be our guests as soon as we're ready," said Imma, as we were about to leave.

"It was a pleasure having both of you, and we'll do it again."

"Shall I take you back to your place?" asked Dave.

"Thank you, I think we can manage. I memorized the streets as we walked here and I had checked the map at home before we came."

"Shoshi," Imma said on the way home, "I know you were trying to be nice to Adele when you said 'I can always change my mind.' Rambam is the school you're going to, no if's or but's. So Tuesday you must go with a positive attitude."

"I must go to her school or I won't see her any more. Please."

"Of course, you will. You heard me invite them and they'll still invite us. We go to the same shul. They have youth groups there for after-school activities. So don't worry about seeing her."

"OK," I said, still disappointed. "Do you think what she said is true?"

"I don't know. Different people see things differently. Wait 'til you see for yourself."

I reached out for Imma's hand and felt its warmth and strength.

As I lay down for my Shabbat nap, I became more determined than ever to help Imma. I would be Imma's *shadchan*, her matchmaker. That was my own responsibility, only mine. Would Mr. Tanarof be the right person? He seemed so warm, friendly and happy. Only if Adele's parents were really breaking up. I wouldn't want to hurt my dear friend. Still if he's the kind of man who breaks up families, does Imma need him?

Then I thought of a great idea. I should have thought of it before. I'll go see the rabbi. Rabbi Freiberg should know which men in his congregation are available and unmarried – and not too poor. Now I can close my eyes.

That evening after *havdalah*, I watched television – for the first time. A set came with our rented apartment. I was amazed at all the different channels and variety of programs. I enjoyed the exciting music and some of the humor but the murders and robberies were ugly and silly. And most of the family stories were about broken homes. I didn't need that. I watched because I thought I might learn something. I didn't.

I went to sleep that night disturbed about my conversations with Imma. I'm still angry at her. She could have told me more about her family years ago. I wouldn't have worried so much all this time. I'm surprised she didn't find her own mother, my Savta. Nobody knows what happened to her. Was that the reason she decided to go into Holocaust studies? Could Imma have missed her mother's name among all the records in the Museum of the Diaspora? Or in Yad Vashem? They have thousands and thousands of family trees there. Maybe I'll write to them.

VIII
INVITATIONS

I'm writing letters this Sunday morning, Imma. I'm writing to all my friends and to Abba. You know, once I start school, I won't have much time."

"Go right ahead," Imma called from the kitchen. "I'm very busy today. Remember to check your blue dress. I hope it's not wrinkled or spotted. You don't have too many nice dresses now, mostly skirts. We'll have to wait until our lift shows up. I called the local office and gave them our new address and telephone number."

"OK, Imma. Can I use your Hebrew typewriter while you're busy? You always tell me how important typing is for high school and college."

'All right, but be careful. Remember I borrowed it until ours arrives."

"Now I can finish my letters. It's time I thanked the girls for their sending-off party and gave them my new address. I must tell Dvorah I always wear my *Mizpah* necklace and think of her. Nobody can take her place."

And Abba. I think I'll give him one last chance. Maybe, just maybe, he would come back to be with us. It's almost time for his yearly conference here, so he won't be coming just for us.

I typed the addresses and piled the envelopes, one on top of the other. Finally, I sealed my last letter and began to put on the stamps.

"Shoshi, it's almost lunch-time. Did you look at your dress?"

I flew to the closet where my dress had been hanging since last Friday. I looked at it, turned it around and sighed with relief. All the wrinkles were gone and there was no blemish or stain – though I wished I had a new dress. .

"Imma, Imma, it'll do. It's almost like new," I shouted.

"I'm happy for you. Come, it's time to eat."

"Imma," I asked, as we were eating, "You told me a lot about Abba but I still don't know exactly why Abba left. Do you hate him?"

"No."

"Did he hate you?"

"No."

"Then I don't understand. I remember how scared I used to be at night. I heard loud voices and pounding coming from your bedroom, like arguments."

"Yes, it was mostly about jobs and money."

"What do you mean?"

"He couldn't keep a job long. Not because he wasn't talented. Say his plans for houses might cost too much and the builder wanted to make them cheaper or not so artistic. Abba would object – and sometimes get violent. He would not allow anyone to change his designs. He would quit and look for another builder. This would happen again and again.

"We never had enough. Abba wanted the money for himself and I needed it for the whole family. I had to take care of all the bills and expenses and save every *agorah* and *shekel*. I never told you I put cardboard in my shoes when they got holes, but you were always neatly dressed.

"And there were other things...."

"Poor Imma, you've been through so much." I walked around the table to Imma and squeezed her tightly and kissed her.

"Still, Abba might get a good job and have money for all of us."

"It's more than that. We talked about it..."

"Maybe he can change." I looked into Imma's eyes pleading. "I'm sure Abba loves us, even if he doesn't buy us any gifts."

The telephone rang.

"Yes, this is Mrs. Bernstein. Mrs. Levin? Oh, yes, I called you last week. You can? That's wonderful. Thank you very much. Yes, she'll be ready, right at the main entrance to the complex. How can I ever thank you. I deeply appreciate what you're doing."

I looked up.

"Let me guess. I'll bet somebody did offer a ride to school, after all."

"Yes, and just in time. You never can tell about people. The children are younger than you. I hope you don't mind."

"That's OK."

"You'll have to be ready early. It may mean waiting outside. Mrs. Levin has two of her own children and picks up three others besides you to make up a full car."

"I'm glad I won't have to walk to school and be tired out on my first morning there."

"And the time to get there and back each day. We have to be grateful."

The phone rang again.

"Thank you, Mrs. Sanders. You are most considerate. We do appreciate it ever so much."

"I can't guess this time, Imma."

"You've heard the saying: 'when it rains, it pours.' Well, Mrs. Sanders thought it would not be fair to ask you to take a taxi from here to Newton where they're having her daughter's bat mitzvah. She's arranged to have one of the parents pick you up. That's something I never expected."

"Imma, you were going to pay for a taxi to take me to the bat mitzvah?"

"Yes, I wouldn't dream of depriving you of your first chance to meet your classmates and make friends."

I guess my Imma is really the greatest. I must promise myself to take a good look around tonight. Who knows what I might find?

It was nearly midnight when our car arrived home. Through the glass entrance I could see Imma watching in the foyer. I got out and waved to the car and a half-dozen hands waved back. Then I waved to Imma as she opened the outer door. I dragged myself in, eyes almost closed...

"How was it?"

"Magnificent," I said, almost swooning into Imma's arms, "Simply magnificent."

One flight up and I collapsed into bed.

IX
SCHOOL FRIENDS

Y ou're lucky school doesn't start until tomorrow," Imma said
to me the next morning. "You're in no shape to go today."

"Neither are all the other girls and boys at the bat
mitzvah, Imma. Some were still there when we left."

"Now, you have a whole day to tell me about it."

"It was lovely. Dalia is as fine as her mother, soooo nice. She
made me sit near her at the class table. Some of the other girls got
jealous. It wasn't my fault. Most were OK. I met Andrea, Gabby,
Jacqueline – she calls herself Jackie – and Mindy. They were the
friendliest...

"Oh, I'm embarrassed to tell you. An older man came over to
me and said he would love to have me for a daughter. I turned
real red. I don't know why he said it. I thought everybody heard
him and was watching me. He told he was a teacher somewhere.
I'm not sure if he said Rambam or some other name. Maybe he'll
be my teacher. His name's Mr. Graubard or Dr. Graubard. I don't
remember which. That's not all. One of his sons, the younger one,
will be in my class. The older son's away at a yeshiva someplace.
Anyway, Mr. Graubard brought him over to meet me. Yoni didn't
seem to be too interested in meeting me, but he was polite. Maybe

he was just shy. I suppose I was, too. He seemed nice, and I liked the way he spoke. His voice sounds smooth and musical. His father left us alone to talk, but soonI don't know why – we ran out of words... So we went back to the class table."

"Were the girls dressed like you?"

"Some were show-offs, looked like they were wearing their mother's evening gowns. Most wore party dresses that looked real expensive. I didn't care; it didn't bother me. I had a great time anyway. I enjoyed the music and dancing and everything."

"Are you glad you went?"

"Oh. Imma, of course. Most were nice to me. When I go to school tomorrow, I won't feel alone after all."

The ride to school took less than ten minutes, long enough to make friends, young friends. I sat in the back with Mrs. Levin's two twin seven-year-old sons, Michael and Gavriel, who both had radiant red hair.

"My two little angels," she called them.

During the trip I talked to them slowly in Hebrew so they would understand.

"Thank you, Shoshanna. I'm glad you spoke to them. If we keep this up every morning, they can become real Israelis without a tutor," she laughed.

I got out first and helped the smaller children out, one by one, so Mrs. Levin could stay at the driver's seat.

"Thank you so much for taking me," I said.

"It was a pleasure to have you along. Same time tomorrow," Mrs. Levin said and waved good-bye.

Inside the central hall hundreds of students, from kindergarteners to high school seniors, were milling around. I felt good to fit right into the middle of them, not the smallest and not the biggest. They were greeting each other like old friends who had not seen each other in years, hugging and gripping hands, all excited and screaming and glad to be back. They reminded me of flocks of goats I once saw on a kibbutz penned up in a corral running around, jumping all over each other and chewing away with their jaws in constant motion. But goats could not shout so loud. Within that big crowd I couldn't find my new friends of last night. Would they be late for school, like Adele and I were for shul? I heard they have services every morning.

A bell rang out. The clamor stopped all at once – like magic! Everyone began to walk ahead down a corridor. It was like goats suddenly changing into sheep that were trudging along a narrow path between two high fences. I followed the older students into a large side room where there was an ark in front. By the time I got in I saw several of my new friends sitting on a back row holding prayer books. They motioned for me to join them and moved over to make space. It felt good to be accepted so quickly.

The rest of the day went by fast. I followed my schedule and met the teachers in every classroom and received an outline for the whole year in every subject. I tried to listen very carefully. I took notes on the course requirements and the reading assignments. All the books I needed were ready. There were too many to take home at one time. I wondered if I would have enough time to do all the work the teachers wanted.

My friends were divided up between the regular and honors groups. Still, I'd see some of them in each class, especially Yoni, who told me he was in all the honors subjects. We all ate together. During lunch I sat down next to Jackie who was very vivacious and liked to talk. Dalia acted like she was still the hostess.

"The drinks are on me today, just today," she said. "Are all of you ordering chocolate milk?"

"Except me," called out Mindy. "My mother says I'm allergic to chocolate – I think she means addicted. She made me promise; so, today, make mine white."

"Shoshanna," Jackie said, "I saw how serious you were in science class. Don't worry about the assignments. It's not going to take you or me the three hours they say you need for all your studies." .

"Are you sure? I was already dreading unfinished work and sleepless nights."

"No," she laughed, "they just want to be tough the first days of school, to impress us."

"Thanks, you make me feel so much better. I was scared. By the way, my friends in Israel call me 'Shoshi.'"

"Oh," Jackie said, "that's cute. I like it."

I had three assignments the first day. I had to read the first chapter in my life-science book, write a short paper in English about my summer experiences, and review the first portion of this week's *sedrah* for Torah class.

"Imma, it wasn't too bad," I said when I got home. "It's a long day but, somehow, you don't feel it. You can make friends there. The teachers are nice. They're firm – you can't fool around in class – but warm – and most of them listen to what we say. I think it's going to be OK."

"Shoshi, you make me feel good. I was really worried about the big change for you from a short to a long school day with more subjects and more study and homework. It worked out better than I expected."

"But it's only five days. Anyway, I'm famished. What's for dinner?"

"Your favorite: spaghetti and meatballs."

"Great, where's a fork?"

"Shoshi," Imma said after dinner, "I'll be coming home late tomorrow. I was asked to lead a seminar in the afternoon and give a lecture tomorrow evening to some graduate students, before classes begin. So, don't worry."

"Imma, where will you eat? You're not taking along a lunch like me?"

"Not tomorrow. There's a Hillel House where I can get kosher meals in the afternoon and evening. It's no problem."

"Looks to me, Imma, like once we both get started on our school work, we'll only be meeting at dinner time and weekends."

"That might be," Imma smiled, "and we'll have so much to share when we do get together."

"Since you mentioned 'lecture,' you might like to know that Mrs. Katz asked me to give a talk about my school work in Israel and the activities of my Bnei Akiva group."

"That's wonderful! I know you can do a fine job."

"Well, I better get back to my studies," I continued.

"You know, Imma, I have so many books – about twenty – not counting the library books I have to read – I could not bring them all home at one time. I'm sure glad there's a book case in my room. Are you going to study, too?"

"Yes. I have to prepare a syllabus for each course I'm giving."

"A syllabus?" I burst out. "That's the word they used for our year's outline in each class. There's a lot of work in those outlines."

I got down to my schoolwork. I wanted to make a good impression on my teachers, to prove myself. I was the last one accepted for the class, which took it over the limit of thirty-six students. Still, the class wasn't really that large. They did split up. Only about half of the group was in any classroom at the same time.

A class of eighteen or twenty is neat. You can ask questions and get more attention than with forty in the room. How lucky I was, I thought to myself, that Imma and Abba had encouraged me to write English letters to their friends from the United States who had visited us in Israel. By the time I finished my reading, I was nodding over my book and my writing was scrawled and illegible.

"You better get to bed, Shoshi. You won't learn any more staying up."

"Good night, Imma. I'm changing for bed right now. I've got lots of exciting things to do tomorrow."

X

HELPING OTHERS

Remember, you have the rest of the spaghetti and meatballs to warm up for dinner tonight. Please, clean up. Don't stay up too late. You need the rest.

"You have your own keys to the building and apartment. Don't lose them or you'll have a hard job getting in. Be sure to lock the door when you have to leave."

"Imma, why must you repeat everything all the time? I CAN remember."

"I worry about you. You're all I have."

"Oh, Imma. You're the world's biggest worrier. I'm going to find a medal for you. If you had someone else around, you wouldn't worry as much about me."

"I think you're a wonderful daughter. I'll be going in a few minutes after I straighten things up." Imma kissed me as I was about to leave.

On the way down to the entrance I realized I had forgotten all about my promise to help Imma. I thought that I would have to get a better look at my teachers. It's a shame Mr. Graubard isn't one of them. Wonder what he does teach.

"We get pleasure out of hearing you speak such a perfect Hebrew," Mrs. Levin said as she was driving. "Please keep it up. The children are getting to like it too."

"Are you sure they don't think I'm making them talk, like a teacher?"

"Children like good teachers."

"I suppose you're right. I know I do."

In school I began to make plans for helping Imma. I thought that I must share my plans with someone. I would need help in finding things out and making decisions. Andrea would probably be the best. She's quieter, more sincere, and understanding. I know she can keep a secret. She ought to know more about the teachers than I do.

I looked for Andrea at services and sat next to her. Then I walked with her to Mr. Hirsh's class. That's where you learn to be a "goody-goody," the girls said.

"You only come here once a week," the teacher spoke in a soft, penetrating voice.. "Yet what we say and discuss here should stay with you every minute of the day and night. We call this subject '*mussar u'middot*,' ethics in English We hope to learn how a person should and can behave, and how to relate to others. Yet we do not tell you what to do. It's up to you to decide; you have the choice.

"Our discussion will be based on selections from our sages. Whenever possible we shall use the original Hebrew. Some of these quotations you may already know, so all the material may not be new. Remember, our purpose is not to learn Hebrew, only to open our minds to new ideas.

"To save time, I passed out text sheets. Yosef, please read the quotation from Hillel and translate."

Yosef read: "If I am only for myself, what am I?"

"Hillel's so right," I said to Andrea as we were leaving the room. "We do very little for others. I don't do enough for my mother, and she does so much for me. It makes me feel guilty."

"Really?" Andrea said.

"You see, my mother and I live alone. She's divorced."

"Oh."

"I'd like to help her. We need a man around, you know. I was wondering about ... about some of the teachers. You know what I mean, don't you?"

"I guess so. I've been here since first grade."

"I was hoping you could you help me."

"Are you sure your mother knows about all this and wants you to do it?"

"It's a secret. She doesn't know about it and I'm sure she wouldn't want me to do it. You're the only person," I said as I turned to face Andrea, "I've told this to. You won't tell anyone about it, will you?"

"Of course not. I'll try to help. It's like a mitzvah, doing something good for others, like Hillel would expect us to. What would you like me to do?"

"I knew I could depend on you. You're the best. Could you find out which men are single? That would be a good beginning."

"All right. I'll call you as soon as I find out for sure. That way it won't look like we're buzzing secrets in school."

"Great. See you at lunch."

After lunch we walked together to Social Studies class. I felt close to Andrea. We shared something special, something important nobody else knew about.

"I have one more requirement to complete this course," Mrs. Katz said, "and that is: Social Service." She wrote the words large on the board.

"It doesn't matter whether you're the best student in class. Without some type of social service you will not get credit for this course.

"To put it another way, it is not enough to know what's wrong with the world. You must do something – even a little – about it.

"We require two hours of community work per week – that's not much – for a period of six weeks, devoted to others without reward, only for the satisfaction of helping our fellow creatures.

"Later you may also be asked to write about your experience. I'm distributing sheets with a list – hospitals, old age homes, schools for the handicapped, and so on. Take the sheets with you and make your choice. Be sure to return them by Friday because we have to make arrangements."

"Isn't it funny, Andrea, how things fit in? This morning Mr. Hirsh discussed doing for others and said it's up to us. We go to Mrs. Katz's class and she tells us to make a choice. It's almost like they planned it together.

"You know, Andrea, I'm beginning to like this school...and the day is over before you know it."

"It sure is, Shoshi. But, by the time I get home, I'm exhausted, and have almost no time left to relax and enjoy things."

I wrinkled my nose. "You're so right." I couldn't tell her that schoolwork didn't tire me out – just worried me.

By the time I got home, I knew I must try harder to help Imma. I could make calls while preparing dinner. I would call the rabbi first. He should know a lot about people. I could catch him at shul. He teaches before evening service.

I called the synagogue on the kitchen phone and held it while I took carrots, lettuce, tomatoes, and cucumbers out of the refrigerator. Then I pitched the earpiece against my shoulder to free my two hands to make a salad.

"Hello, who is it?"

"Rabbi Freiberg?"

"No, it's Mr. Pilchik, the *shammash*."

"May I please speak to Rabbi Freiberg?"

"Why? You sound like a young girl. What's your name?"

"Shoshanna Bernstein. You see, I'm new around here and I need some help."

"All right, hold on and I'll see if he's free."

I finished the salad as I waited. Then I began to warm up my main dish on the stove.

"Hello, this is Rabbi Freiberg. What can I do for you? I'm sorry I had to keep a young lady waiting."

"I don't know if you remember me. I was in shul last Shabbat for the first time and wished you 'Shabbat Shalom' on the way out."

"I'm sure you did. What can I do for you?"

"Well, I have a special problem."

"What is it?"

"You see, my mother and I live alone. She's divorced. We – my mother and I – miss having a man say *kiddush*, *havdalah*, etc. You understand. I was wondering if you know of any man who is single and might wish to marry a wonderful mother. She's pretty and a teacher at Harvard. Everybody likes her. Besides, she knows how to save money."

I thought I heard someone laughing into the phone.

"Fine, I'll be delighted to meet her."

"Could you do me a favor?"

"Yes?"

"Please don't tell her I called."

"Of, course not. You are a most remarkable girl and a fine daughter. I'm looking forward to saying 'Shabbat Shalom' again."

I felt great. I didn't feel alone while eating dinner. The phone rang. I grabbed it.

"Mrs. Bernstein?"

"No, this is Shoshanna."

"Shoshanna, this is Andrea's mother. I spoke to Mrs. Levin about your car pool. I thought you might like to ride with your classmates. We made room for you and switched and I gave her Zelda, my younger daughter."

"Won't Mrs. Levin mind?"

"I'm sure she'll miss you. She told me she would call you later. It works out better this way. Next week when the full schedule begins, the younger children leave school earlier than your class does."

"It will be great riding with Andrea. Thank you very much."

As I hung up, the phone rang once more.

"Hello, this is Mr. Miller. Is this Mrs. Bernstein?"

"No, this is Shoshanna."

"Oh. I live here, too. I saw your name on the school lists. You see my son and daughter go to Rambam. May I speak to your mother?"

"She's not in now."

"Please give her my message. I'd like to invite both of you to dinner this Shabbat evening. I'm only two flights up."

"I'll certainly tell her to call as soon as I speak to her. Thank you."

Another miracle! A man is inviting Imma to dinner – and I just finished calling the rabbi. I'm happy there's no homework tonight – except some reading. I better clean up this mess first. Then, I'll read in bed.

I fell asleep with my book open and light on – and never saw Imma that evening...

XI

My Sudden Fall

Imma, I'm riding with Andrea... and I'm so sorry I fell asleep last night. You had a message from a Mr. Miller who lives here. He invited us to Friday night dinner. Could we go, please?" I looked into Imma's eyes, pleading.

"I'm so happy you left everything spotless last night, although I know you must have been tired All right, I'll call Mr. Miller to thank him for his Shabbat invitation. It's nice to have friends in the same apartment building. How lucky you are to ride with Andrea."

I'm glad Imma feels so good this morning, I thought on my way downstairs: Imma doesn't know about my plans. I must keep working on them.

As I entered the car to sit beside Andrea, I had a surprise. Mindy and Jackie were in the back. They must be friends from way back – and they want me to be with them!

"Do you get together all the time? I'm so glad to ride with you."

"We live near each other and our mothers take turns. It's easy to pick you up on the way in," Andrea offered.

"It's good being with you. Thanks."

When we arrived at school we saw Dalia and Gabby running to join us.

"Anybody decide about their 'social service'?" Jackie blurted out.

"I'd like to get started right away, before we get loaded down with tests and tough assignments."

"How about working with kids?" asked Mindy. "We could share their chocolates and candies."

"Here, you sweet thing, have a cherry drop," said Dalia.

I hesitated, then felt I had to say something.

"I just thought I might try an old age home. You see, I never knew my grandparents.

My own parents barely saw theirs. So, I thought it'd be nice to make-believe, like taking care of my own grandmother."

Dalia gave me a weird look. "Old folks are kooky." Then, smiling, she added, "Maybe it's a good idea; they could use our help. I'll try it, too."

Gabby grinned.

"I guess you guys don't know that Jackie's brother works at the Golden Age Retirement Home part-time and on Sundays with his two friends. I saw them at her house; they're real cute. You should see them."

"Is that true, Jackie? Why didn't you tell us?" Mindy asked.

"Oh, I just wanted you to make up your own minds," Jackie said.

"That settles it. I'm going for those old people – kooky or not."

Everyone's eyes brightened up, all excited.

"Then let's all go." Andrea said. "I'm handing in my sheet now. We might begin this Sunday. It's the only day we have open, anyway."

"Maybe they'll give us time off from school," Gabby suggested.

"Are you kidding?" We all laughed.

"I can dream, can't I?" Mindy retorted, with a broad grin.

"Besides," I added, "what good would it do? We'd still be

responsible for our missed assignments and have to work twice as hard."

Before school began the six of us went to Mrs. Katz's room and gave her our social service sheets. We had no class with her that day.

"I'm glad we finally decided," Jackie said, running the back of her right hand over her forehead. "Now we'll wait to hear."

That afternoon I went to science lab for the first time. It looked just perfect for making experiments: black tabletops, electric and gas outlets, shelves full of insect, plant and other specimens, and roll-up charts, like window shades on the walls, one above the other. Inside glass cases I saw lines of microscopes, measuring cups, beakers and siphons – more items than I could count. I looked around. Everybody was admiring the room. I bet it was recently done over.

Mr. Eisen stood behind a demonstration table in the front of the room.

"Good morning and welcome to our brand-new science lab. I'm sure we're going to spend many hours of fun and learning here. We only have two periods a week and cannot afford to waste time. You must be prepared to start work the moment you arrive. Some experiments require demonstration, so you will have to observe me carefully. Others do not. You have your text and workbook to guide you.

"If you have any questions, please ask – now or later."

Everybody looked at everybody else; no one spoke.

"To make your work easier and avoid errors, you will have partners. Remember: always take notes. Each experiment has to be written up. For me," Mr. Eisen pounded with his fist on the table, "the regular weekly assignments properly completed mean more than a high mark on a one-time final exam.

"Now for your partners. When I finish reading the names,

move to your assigned table and stand by your partner. Jonathan Aaronson and Harvey Milgram, Table 1; Shoshanna Bernstein and Johnnie Graubard, Table 2; "

I was stunned. Was Yoni - -it must be his name – my partner? I got hot and flushed; my hands felt clammy. As I took a step, I tripped over my feet and my books flew from my arms into the air. I fell flat on the floor, bruising my left knee and elbow and scraping my hands.

My eyes were getting moist. A crowd gathered around. Two girls raised me up and dusted off my skirt. Others collected my books.

"Are you hurt? Do you want to see the nurse?"

"No, no, I'm all right," I whispered, though I didn't feel that way. I was all shook up and needed time to get my balance. My knee twinged. Slowly I limped over to Table 2. Yoni was there.

"Sorry I couldn't get over in time to help you. How do you feel?"

"Better now, nothing serious." I smiled, still uneasy and embarrassed because of my clumsiness. During the session most of the pain left me but my head was still throbbing.

As we left the room, Yoni remarked:

"We should be able to work well together on our experiments. I'll be happy to offer you all the help I can."

I looked up at him. I felt a headache coming on. What does he mean he'll help me? Who does he think he is?

"What makes you think I'll need help and have to ask you?"

Yoni started to falter.

"Well...I really didn't mean it the way it sounded. I'm sorry."

"Besides, what *is* your name? Your father said your name was `Yoni.' Mr. Eisen called you `Johnnie.' Which is it?"

"Well...if you want to know the truth, more people call me Johnnie than Yoni, which is really short for Yohanan. When I was young... in the first grade, the kids began to tease me. I was very shy then. They called me Johnnie to get me angry. It caught on and I was stuck with it. Now our teachers use it. At first I was annoyed but I really don't mind now. You can use the one you like best."

"Which one do you like better?" I was sorry that I been so awful to him.

Yoni looked directly at me. "Yoni."

"Then, that's what I'll call you. My friends call me Shoshi."

"Then, that's what I'll call you," Yoni said, echoing my words.

Imma was at home when I arrived.

"I didn't expect to see you so early, Imma."

"You know if I were to stay late, I would let you know. Besides, we haven't had time to discuss much in two days."

"Yes, Imma, you're so sweet." I wrapped my arms about Imma and kissed her.

"That was an unusually warm and tight hug. Any special reason?"

"No, in fact, I'm bruised – on my left side – and I scraped my hands."

"What happened?"

"I tripped and fell to the floor."

"Come, we'll get you washed up and put on alcohol."

After my treatment, I said quietly:

"You were right, Imma. Guess what. The boy I met at the bat mitzvah, Yoni Graubard, is my science partner. I think he's very nice since I came to know him better. It's funny that the kids call him `Johnnie.'"

"Why?"

"It's a long story. Tell you another time. But...you know something funny? I acted mean to him – and I don't know why."

Imma didn't answer; she just smiled.

"All right. About the Shabbat invitation. I called Mr. Miller and accepted his offer for Shabbat evening."

"His wife and children live with him, too?"

"No, he's divorced. His children are nine and ten."

Oh, boy, this is great. Imma's going to a man's apartment for dinner and she'll have to invite him back. Now, we're getting somewhere. I'll play with the children so they can be together.

XII
A MAN FOR MY MOTHER

Some students have already handed in their social service
sheets," Mrs. Katz announced, "so I was able to speed up
their arrangements. All others must be in by the end of this
day. I would like to see the early birds at the end of this period."

She smiled, looking in our direction.

When we saw Mrs. Katz at the end of that period she was happy
to tell us our assignment.

"I arranged for you girls to be volunteer aides at the Golden Age
Residential Home.

Your appointment is for 10 am this coming Sunday. I hope it's
not too soon for you.

"When you get there – I'll give you directions – ask for the head
nurse, Mrs. Rosenthal. She'll give you your assignments. Those
who went there in past years gained from the experience, and
enjoyed it. I'm sure you will, too. Thanks for being so prompt."

"We hope so," said Gabby. "I'm going to miss my one free day
each week. Let's get over with it as soon as we can."

Mrs. Katz looked at us, smiled again, but said nothing.

"Mother will be happy to drive us over," Andrea offered.

"Not this time," Dalia interrupted. "My mother can drive our station wagon. It can hold all of us."

"Fine with me. No squeezing," Andrea said. The girls laughed.

Imma stayed home Friday. And school was always dismissed early that day.

While I like to learn, school can be boring at times as some teachers keep droning away in a monotone that can put a tiger to sleep. And so much repetition... it gets annoying.

So I was happy to get home and try to be of some use by helping in the clean-up. In Israel, when I got home by noon, we worked together to make our apartment spick-and-span "Shabbat clean" – washing, dusting, mopping and polishing the floors, silverware, candlesticks and *kiddush* cups. We would put away the daily dishes and take out our special sets for Shabbat, holidays and special occasions. Those sets were coming by boat. Imma bought new plain dishes in a supermarket sale on Harvard Street. We had brought along the unbreakables, like our good silverware, in a large container. As usual, Imma bought flowers for our vase while I polished the *kiddush* cups and candle sticks and placed them on the Shabbat cloth. The table looked so warm and bright, a sign of a happy family.

"Imma, we're having a busy weekend. We're guests tonight and going to shul tomorrow morning, baby-sitting tomorrow night and, Sunday, visiting an old age home."

"You mean *you*, don't you, Shoshi? *You're* having a busy weekend. And what's this about visiting an old age home?" she asked.

"Oh, that's a school assignment, my 'social service,' they call it. Maybe I'll find a grandmother there. Who knows?" I smiled.

Imma looked at me quizzically but was mum. I laughed and hugged her.

On his way back from shul that evening, Mr. Miller knocked at our door. We all went up together to his apartment. It was all lit up, with a Shabbat table set for five. I was attracted to the tablecloth.

It was embroidered with eagles and lions, candlesticks and cups, tablets of stone and Torahs – all in gold, blue and white threads.

The food was delicious. I was surprised a man could prepare and serve such an excellent meal. He would not let us do anything. We were guests, he said. We all sang *zemirot* together. The children, Edith and Robert, knew them all.

After dinner we all entered the living room. The children brought out their games: cards and checkers, dominoes and dice, and little colored plastic pieces for make-believe money. I was glad to play with them. I wanted Imma and Mr. Miller to be able to talk by themselves and get to know each other. I was trying hard so Imma couldn't say she was alone.

"Imma, I was surprised tonight. First time I saw a man really make a great full-course dinner with all the trimmings: a special salad, roast chicken, and apple pie. How did he do it?"

"Don't judge by your father, who couldn't boil an egg. Many men like to be in the kitchen. They say the best chefs in restaurants and hotels are men. Still, he tells me he's very busy. He probably took a day off to get ready and bought some prepared food. I'm sure he didn't bake the pie."

"What's he like?"

"He's intelligent and pleasant. He owns some kind of factory. His wife left him for another man and deserted her own children. He was very disturbed. He moved here recently to start all over again. He's only divorced six months and is trying to forget what happened. It's good we joined them for dinner. He needs company. Remember, all this is only between us."

"Sure, Imma. Do you think he'd like to get married again?"

Imma knit her eyebrows and looked at me strangely.

"What are you dreaming up? Don't even think of it."

After morning services, I pulled Imma over to meet the rabbi.

"Shabbat Shalom, Rabbi Freiberg. I'm Shoshanna Bernstein and

I want you to meet my mother."

"Shabbat Shalom, Shoshanna. I'm happy to meet you, Mrs. Bernstein. We've never met before. You must be new here."

"Yes, we are. We recently arrived from Israel. We do have long-time friends here, the Tanarofs."

"Oh. They just returned from Israel. I think Dr. Tanarof had a sabbatical there."

"He was doing research in my department at the Hebrew University."

"Then, you're a professor, too. Your specialty?"

"Holocaust studies, principally."

"Sounds impressive. It's one subject we could all learn more about and must never forget. Would you care to speak before our men's or women's groups?"

Imma smiled. "I'd be honored to. Perhaps at a later date."

"Of course. I realize you're just getting organized. My wife will call to invite you to dinner, as we do all our new congregants. Shabbat Shalom."

I found the Miller family in the outside courtyard. It looked like they were waiting to walk home with us. I held the hands of the children.

Our families began to separate as we entered our apartment building. I became upset. I buzzed into Imma's ear.

"Let's invite them for *kiddush*."

"No."

"Please, Imma, they look so sad."

"No."

"You're unfair. I think they expect it."

"Oh, all right."

I felt so good. For once I had won a battle with Imma while fighting for her.

"What a lovely apartment you have, Mrs. Bernstein. And such tasty honey cake, made by the hands of a real *balebusteh*."

Imma blushed and turned her head to the side.

"I'm glad you liked it. I prefer baking my own though I've been very busy."

"I understand. It's a big change from Israel."

After they left, I helped Imma clean up. I was eager to learn more.

"Imma, what do you think of him now? I liked his *kiddush* melody."

"Well, you always recognize a good voice when you hear one. Anyway, every time we're together he tells me more about himself. He's really a fine person: trustworthy, hard-working and loves children. He was shocked by his wife's leaving and divorcing him and he's very concerned about his children. I think his wife was a lot younger than he was."

"Does it make a difference?"

"Only if she fell in love with a younger man. Probably – I'm guessing - -I really shouldn't - -she probably admired Mr. Miller as a successful business man and a person who treated her well. Later she found someone more youthful and exciting. He's very eager to get married soon, because he feels he can`t be both father and mother. I'm sure he wants a whole family for the sake of his children."

"You don't think this is the right time?"

"Do you mean for him or for me?"

"Well, both of you."

"Shoshi, please, don't rush me. I'm too busy to even think of marriage."

"Then why do you keep complaining you have no one, you're all alone?"

I noticed Imma clamp her jaws and tighten up. She did not answer. I could see Imma didn't mean it. She does need someone. I must keep trying. I think I'm getting somewhere. It may take a little while.

After *havdalah* Imma walked me over to Mrs. Levin's home on Babcock Street. As I pressed the bell button, the door snapped open and two twin red mops of hair popped out chanting: "*Shavua tov.*"

XIII
A New Adventure

At 9:45 a.m. our car approached the Golden Age Residential Home near Hammond Pond Parkway. In the distance a stone mansion arose, set within acres of green fields, tall trees and flower gardens. I enjoyed the drive on the long curving road leading from the highway to the building entrance.

We all ran up the steps and rushed to the office. Nurse Rosenthal was there expecting us.

"I'm delighted to see you all, but you don't have to be out of breath. Please come in and be comfortable. This is our conference room where we discuss the welfare and treatment of our residents. That's really what you'll be doing. You'll be improving the well-being of our senior citizens.

"How will you achieve all that? Just by being here you make a tremendous difference. You are young and bright, full of life and spirit. That's great medicine. You make our residents feel happier, younger and more active. You can comfort those who need it with smiles and songs, tell them stories or simply talk about what's going on outside. You can take them in their wheel chairs or walkers or by supporting them to the dining hall at lunch time or to the TV room or to the Sunday afternoon programs we have in our auditorium.

"You see, you can do things we can't. We cannot afford the time or supply the personnel to do all the things I mentioned, and they are so important.

"Are there any questions so far?" No one spoke up at first.

"How do we get started?" Andrea asked after a pause.

Nurse Rosenthal smiled and answered, "I'm glad to find you all so eager. We will assign each of you to one resident. You'll all be on the same floor, close to one another. We'll give you notes on the history and health of your resident so you'll know something about her: her family, jobs she had, her interests and hobbies, her education, how much you can expect her to do, and so on.

"We'd like you to start about ten in the morning. By then, they've had their breakfast, they have rested in their rooms, and they should be getting around. First, you can just talk to your resident to get her confidence and 'warm' her up. That way she'll forget herself and open her eyes to the world.

"Some are more alert than others. In fine weather, you can take them out into our beautiful gardens and sit and talk with them there. In bad weather, we have a large enclosed area with glass doors where they come to look out at nature. As you get on, you will figure out what they enjoy doing or hearing about: the weather, your school, your family or hers, sports or just plain stories. Some like to play games or work in crafts.

"Lunch is 11:30 to 12:30. You'll be able to take them to the dining hall. You do not stay there yourself. They take their own meals.

"After lunch we take those who wish to the Sunday afternoon show in our auditorium. We have professional and amateur performers who donate their time, including musicians and singers, actors and dancers. You might enjoy seeing the program. For a change we may show a film but not too often.

"If you decide to stay for the afternoon, we can provide, in our own staff dining room, a kosher lunch.

"How do you feel all about all this?"

I looked around at the other girls. They were looking about, too. After a while, Jackie perked up.

"It sounds great to me. I'm for staying from ten to... let's say... about two. By that time, the show should be over."

"What do you other girls think?" the nurse asked. I nodded with the rest.

"How do you manage during the week?" Gabby asked.

"We get college students, retired people and others. Sunday is harder for us. Everybody wants to enjoy Sunday with their own families and friends. That's why we're so happy you could come today.

"Is everything clear? We shall not keep you long today. Now, I'll give each of you a sheet with notes about your resident and her first name – that's how we call them. We would like you to read it and leave it here. We know this information will help you in working with your resident.

"We call you volunteer aides. You will wear blue-and-white armbands and receive a certificate when your service is completed. Any final questions?

"No? Then, after you've finished reading, I'll show you our Home. You should be on your way in about half-an-hour."

"May I call my mother to pick us up then?" Dalia asked.

"Of course. You can make your call here."

In the little time we had left, the head nurse took us for a brief tour of the first floor. We walked through the well-lit dining hall with its brightly painted walls and tables for four, decorated with flower vases; then we saw the two modern kitchens, a large auditorium with its well-equipped stage and a small chapel adorned with glass-stained windows.

"How did it go, Shoshi? " Imma asked when I returned at noon.

"Fine. It's a new experience in helping others. We're going there Sundays from ten to two."

"Isn't that a lot of time?"

"It's a school assignment. We'd rather get it done earlier than later, before we have to study for tests on the weekends."

"Anyway, I'm glad you didn't stay late today. I planned for us to go to the Boston Commons for the Walking Tour. Would you like that?"

"Great."

"Only the two of us, out in the open enjoying the end of summer weather while learning some history."

That night I tried to remember what I had read at the Home. I was going to meet a new-old grandmother, well, actually an adopted Savta. I would care for her. Her name was Sadie, born overseas, lost her family, including a baby girl, in the Holocaust, came to America with a close friend and spent most of her life working hard. Now, she was resting and enjoying her golden years at the Residents Home. Did she like people or not? Was she happy or sad? Did she like to play games or listen to stories? Was this the beginning of a new adventure, a new mystery? One thing was for sure. She needed a grandchild – and I was the one.

XIV
MEETING A SPECIAL PERSON

This was a gloomy week. The clouds would not budge and the skies remained dark. And that was just the way I felt – gloomy. Nothing was happening and time was passing by. Nobody was calling me back. I went to the mailbox after school and in the evening but there was nothing for me. I guess it was too soon to expect letters from overseas. Imma was worried about the Holidays three weeks ahead of us: losing time from her work, preparing all the meals, buying clothes for both of us – and still being alone. Maybe she felt bad, like I did, about not being able to build a succah.

I'd been working and waiting, and the more I waited the more I worked. And I didn't know what I was waiting for. In Israel the phone and doorbell were always ringing. Schoolwork is all I really do well – but that doesn't mean I have to love it. Maybe I'm studying too hard, but I like it better than housework, which I hate. I enjoyed my writing: the science report on the plants of Israel, my experience at the dig near Akko, and the story I made up about King Saul from the First book of Samuel. They looked real neat on the printed sheets. My classmates didn't say much about them, but the teachers seemed to like them.

I have to be careful with Imma these days. She's very angry with me. It's not because of Mr. Miller, who calls her once in a while to say hello and likes to walk home with her from shul. She won't let me do baby-sitting for his kids. She says she needs me Friday afternoons to help at home.

It's mostly about the computer. I used it to type those reports, and it took me such a long time. She blamed me because it was not working right. It held up her project and she had to waste time and spend money fixing it. It was not my fault. It got jammed up as I was using it. I don't know what happened.

Or maybe it's something else? I know she doesn't like me to stay up very late. She worries too much. When I'm tired out from study, I sleep like a log.

Yoni is quiet these days. He doesn't say much. I don't know why. We both work together and I try to be nice and help him. I try hard to get our experiments and workbooks done on time. I don't know if I'm imagining it but my friends are quieter, too, these days – at least when they're near me. I wanted to study with them for the math test – percent, ratio, proportion and simple equations – but they said it was better to study alone. Besides, they said that I lived too far away to get together easily.

I studied late that night; it was worth it. Next day I got an almost perfect paper, second best in the class.

I feel all alone now and I don't know why I read and look at television. Imma made me promise only one half-hour during the week and no more than two hours on weekends.

The bright spot in my life is being with Sadie, but I don't call her that. I think the other girls feel the same about their residents and are always eager to be with them.

Sadie was sad at first and, like me, all alone. I decided to make us into a family. I didn't think it was right to call her Sadie. She was old enough to be my mother's mother. I told her that right away:

"My name's Shoshanna. You can call me Shoshi, like all my

friends do. I know the nurses call you by your first name; I can't do that. I never had a grandmother and need one. I hope you need a grandchild. I'll call you Grandma Sadie. Is that all right with you?"

Sadie smiled at me. Her eyes twinkled.

"Only if I can call you `grandchild.'"

She spoke in a foreign accent. I could not tell where it was from.

"That's great. In that case, could I also call you Savta? That's grandmother in Hebrew?"

I smiled back.

"Oh, you know Hebrew?"

"Yes, I was born in Israel and just came from there."

"Oh, my. And you speak such good English, too."

"Yes, we spoke it at home."

I saw she was starting to look happier and stronger.

"It's a beautiful day outside, Savta. Would you like to go into the garden?"

"I'd love to, grandchild. Because you're here, I'm going to try to go without my walker."

She bent over to hold onto the railing along the wall with her right hand and took my arm with her left. We walked slowly until we reached the garden door. I saw her raise her head and straighten her back. Step-by-short-step we went on. It was a good feeling to have somebody by your side who needed and wanted your help. We sat down on the curved wooden benches around the circular drive.

"And where do you live now, my angel?"

I was prepared for that question. I told her about our home in Brookline and my mother and the school I go to and what we learn there. She listened closely. It was easy talking to her. Then she asked me another question:

"And your family? How long were they in Israel?"

"We're Americans. My parents got married and went on aliyah. I was the one born in Israel. My mother told me I'm still an American citizen."

"You're all Americans and your parents went on aliyah. That's very good."

"Now, Savta, tell me about yourself: where you're from and what you did."

She looked up at me puzzled.

"You really want to know?"

"Yes. I'm very curious. After all, you're part of my family. You're all I have besides my parents." I tried to look serious.

She smiled again and I smiled back.

"Already, I feel very close to you. We are going to be very good friends. I don't have any family either. You're my only *einikel*, my only grandchild."

For the first time, Sadie laughed aloud.

"You know," she said, "there are people here who have lots of relatives who never visit. I hope we see each other more."

"Oh, Savta. I'm going to visit you every week – even if I have a test on Monday."

She tried to hug me but couldn't; so I hugged her. Slowly we walked back to her table in the dining room.

"Have a good appetite," I said. "I'll see you in the lounge after lunch."

"I'll be waiting."

After my lunch with the girls – it was exciting to eat with all the important people of the Home – Sadie was there waiting for me in a corner of the lounge near the window.

"Shoshi, did you have a good lunch? I haven't enjoyed a Sunday meal so much in a long time. And I want you to know. I walked here by myself!"

During the show I sat down next to Sadie holding her hand in mine. We joined in when the singer on the stage had a "sing-along" with the audience. First he taught the words to each song and then the tune. It was fun.

On the drive home, Mindy remarked: "They really need us. We're really helping them to enjoy living."

"I'll bet they haven't had friends like us visiting them in years," Jackie said.

"You're right, Jackie. I felt funny calling a person old enough to be my grandmother by her first name," I said.

"I guess they get used to it. Everybody does it. Maybe they feel closer that way," Gabby said.

"I just couldn't do it. I made her my grandmother."

"I remember your telling us you might do that when we decided to work here," Andrea added.

Nobody said anything else on the way home. I guess we were all thinking.

XV
A GIFT OF LOVE

Another week went by. I was getting desperate. I just couldn't wait any longer to find out what was happening with my plans to help Imma. The world outside wasn't answering. Only my schoolwork was left to keep me busy, and Savta Sadie to make me feel good. Everything else was tumbling down on my head.

Imma looked sad these days. It couldn't be the computer anymore because it was fixed. I think she has many things on her mind and no one to share them with. I was still waiting for my calls.

I decided not to wait any more. I called up Rabbi Freiberg on Wednesday, when Imma stays late at Harvard. I called just before the afternoon service.

"I know why you're calling, Shoshanna. I'm still looking around for the right person for your mother. She's like you, very special. So far I haven't found him. You never know when he may turn up. Remember, we plan to invite both of you to Shabbat lunch."

"Thank you for trying," I answered.

His words did not make me feel better. I called up Andrea.

"Hiya, Andrea. Any good news for my mother?"

"Sorry I didn't call you earlier. I suppose you realized you didn't hear from me because I couldn't find what you wanted. I checked everyone out."

"I was afraid of that. Guess there's no hope."

"Unless the school gets other teachers. We got a problem. The new teachers are too young and the older teachers are married."

"No exception?"

"Yes, one. Someone you know, Dr. Graubard. He's not at Rambam, only comes to teach a special course to seniors on philosophy."

"What do you mean?"

"He's a professor at the Hebrew College."

"Wonderful. What's wrong with that?"

"Nothing. You see, he just lost his wife about a year ago."

"That's terrible."

"It's worse. She was sick for quite a while and he was devoted to her."

"That's a shame. At least, he's not alone. He has two sons."

My mind flashed back to my first meeting with Dr. Graubard and his words to me.

"I still wonder why he said that," I whispered to myself.

"Shoshi, why are you whispering? Who said what?" asked Andrea.

"Oh, nothing."

"Shoshi, what was it?"

"I'll tell you because I trust you but, please, don't tell anyone."

"Of course I won't but say it already."

"Remember Dalia's bat mitzvah? Dr. Graubard was there. He walked up to me and said he'd like to have a daughter like me, whatever that means. I don't know why he said it."

"Oh."

"Don't mention it to the other girls. No one knows this except my mother."

"I won't."

Still, I felt very low, very disappointed. I'm not succeeding with anything or anybody except Savta Sadie.

When we arrived the following Sunday, Nurse Rosenthal took me aside.

"Sadie is in her room. She had a little fall and got bruised. No bones were broken. At her age, however, we thought she ought to rest up today. You can stay with her there. We'll bring up lunch for both of you."

A shock jolted me. My head pained. I grasped my forehead with my palms.

"How did it happen?" I must have screamed. "Tell me what happened."

Nurse Rosenthal put her arm around me, trying to soothe me, and smiled.

"You won't believe it. She was making something for you in the crafts room and slipped off a chair."

"I must go up." Slipped off a chair? Like when I tripped in the lab. I guess when people get excited something happens to them. When I peeked in the doorway, to my surprise, Sadie was laughing and holding her arms out to me. I ran over, happy to find her in such a good mood, and embraced her.

"I was so worried when I heard about your accident. How do you feel?"

"It was nothing. Only a few scratches. They think I'm hurt and too weak to walk. So, I'll rest for a while. I'm glad you're here. Sit here beside me. I have something to show you. Here." She patted the bed.

She took a small tapestry out of a brown bag beside her.

"Do you like it? I wanted to make a garden. It's supposed to be a green grass field with your name in red and yellow like flowers."

I looked at it, amazed and delighted.

"It's beautiful! For me? The first gift I ever received from a Savta. Thank you."

I hugged her all I could and kissed her on the cheek.

"I'm going to hang it up in my room, right above my desk. Every time I sit down to study, I'll look up and it'll make me feel good."

"Now, before lunch comes," Savta said, "I'm going to tell you a little about myself. I wasn't sure what to say last time. I never told you, but you reminded me right away of the girl I lost, though she was much younger. I was taken to a Nazi work camp. There we worked long hours and had a little watery soup and a piece of bread to eat each day. I was strong and managed to live, and I tried to help others want to live.

"I was saved by the American army and came to the United States with a friend who had relatives in this country."

She stopped and took a long breath. Telling about herself excited her and wore her out.

"You don't have to talk any more now. We'll have lots of time to talk. The time has come for resting."

I soothed her arms and forehead.

After we enjoyed a hot lunch together, I said to Savta Sadie,"Savta, I'll tell you stories, true stories. Have you ever been to Jerusalem? No? I think it's the only modern city with a smaller, older city inside. The Old City is beautiful. It has a high stone wall all around it, with seven entrances.

"We like to enter through the Jaffa Gate when we go there. That's the way we reach the Kotel. Some call it the Western Wall. It's faster to walk through the Arab shuk or marketplace. You can buy all kinds of souvenirs there, if you wish, made of metal or wood or leather. Most tourists buy things. We don't. One reason is we visit the Western Wall on Shabbat and holidays and don't carry any money with us."

"You observe the Shabbat? You're a granddaughter after my own heart."

"I don't deserve any credit. All my friends do, too."

"Sorry to hear about Sadie getting hurt," Dalia said, as we were about to go.

"She seems to be getting over it and in good spirits. I'm happy about that."

I was not in good spirits on the drive home. I was embarrassed about the tapestry. I hid it in my pocket so the girls wouldn't ask questions. Besides, it was a present from my Savta Sadie to me. No one else had to know.

Poor Savta. She lost her baby. She must really miss not having children.

Look how she wants to be close to me.

XVI
GUILTY

In my room I looked at the tapestry again. It was small but lovely, and my adopted Savta Sadie made it just for me. Imma was not in the mood to see or appreciate it. I put it away in my blouse drawer before hanging it up.

After our Monday dinner I decided to tell Imma about Savta.

"Imma, I have something sad to tell you about the Holocaust. Savta Sadie lost a baby girl in a concentration camp. I felt so bad for her. And something else. Don't say anything to anyone. Someone told me that Dr. Graubard's wife became ill and died last year."

"I feel very sorry about what happened to Savta Sadie. It's true about Dr. Graubard's wife. I heard she was a fine person."

"How do you know all this?"

"Dr. Graubard told me."

"He told you? Where, when?"

"At Hillel House."

"You never told me."

"You haven't been in a pleasant mood. I saw no point telling you."

"Imma, I thought you were in a bad mood. That's the kind of news I was waiting to hear."

"What kind of news are you talking about?"

"You know. News that you were not alone any more."

Imma looked at me and laughed.

"Anyway, he teaches at the Hebrew College and has a class in Jewish Thought at Hillel. He eats there on Wednesday evenings. He remembered me from the shul and the class parents' meeting."

"I never knew. You see him regularly, don't you? I bet he takes you home."

"Yes, I guess I've been keeping all this from you because you might get the wrong ideas."

This time I laughed, for the first time in a long while.

"What wrong ideas, Imma? We've kept secrets from each other too long. I want to show you something."

I brought out the tapestry. Imma took it in her hand and ran her fingers over it..

"Let me guess. Savta made it for you – to look like flowers in a garden."

"You're so right! I'm going to hang it up above my desk."

That evening Andrea called.

"Hiya, Andrea. What's up?"

"Nothing. I'd just like a chance to talk to you alone."

"Sure. Where?"

"Well, it's hard at school. The kids get all kinds of ideas if they see two people whispering together. You know."

"How can we arrange it? Sounds important."

"It is. Could I come to your place tomorrow evening?"

"You would? I'd be so happy. You could have dinner with us and stay overnight and we could go to school together in the morning."

"My mother wouldn't let me stay overnight, but I could come for dinner. You see my parents were invited to a gathering a few blocks from your place and I told them I'd rather be with you."

"That's terrific. My mother would love to have you, wouldn't you, Imma?

"Andrea, my mother said yes. We don't have to tell anyone. See you in school."

"I don't know what it's about, Imma, but she sounds serious. It feels great to have a guest in my own home."

Andrea's parents brought her right to the apartment door. As Imma opened it, Mrs. Robinson spoke briefly.

"It's good meeting you, Mrs. Bernstein. We'll have to get together some time. Actually," she looked at her watch, "we're late for dinner. We'll pick you up at 11, Andrea. Have a good time. Thank you for inviting her, Shoshanna."

After dinner, I led Andrea to my room. I showed her the collection of sea shells and rocks I brought from Israel. Then I pointed to my desk wall.

"Here's something special. Savta Sadie made this tapestry for me. It was a real surprise. I was afraid to show it to the other girls, but I didn't want to keep it a secret from you."

"It's beautiful," Andrea said, taking it in her hands. After a short pause, she continued.

"Shoshi, we've shared a lot of things together. There's something I didn't want to keep secret from you."

She looked straight at me and turned serious.

"We're close friends and I think a lot of you. I want to help you."

"Help me? How?"

"Well, the kids feel funny about you, the things you do."

"What do you mean?"

"Like always fighting to be first. Your hand's always up for every new project. You're always ready to answer any question. Your papers are always in ahead of time. If someone makes a mistake, you're ready to correct."

"What's wrong with all that?"

"Everybody thinks you're a show-off, a goody-goody."

"You know I'm not."

"I'm only one person. They figure you're like that because you come from Israel. It gives Israel a bad name. I know you don't want that."

"That makes me real angry. Just because I work hard they don't like it."

"It's not that. They feel you're telling them off: `See what I can do.'"

"You know I don't feel that way. It's the opposite. I'm always scared I won't do as well as all of you or match the rest of my class because you all live here. So I try to do my best and didn't know I was being too good."

"Not everybody takes school so seriously, but everyone needs friends."

"I was feeling good and now I feel sad and ashamed."

"Shoshi, I only came to share with you, to help. I'm sorry if I made you feel bad."

"No, it's not that. I didn't realize people would think I was being pushy just because I was working hard.

"You can change that – if you work hard at it, like you do with school work."

I thought it over and smiled.

"I guess you're right. Maybe I could. Now, I'll let you in on another secret. My mother met Dr. Graubard at Hillel House and has seen him a few times. They seem to get along..."

"Terrific."

Andrea hugged me and I kissed her on the cheek. It was such a warm feeling. It's great to have a special friend all your own.

But I could not forget Andrea's words. She's such a fine friend and did mean to help me. It was late when her parents came. We were both drowsy.

> *I don't understand it. I was lying in bed in the dark just before and now I'm awake. I'm standing in front of a tall desk and a man with glaring eyes is staring at me. I lowered my eyes, afraid.*
>
> *"Look up at me," he thundered.*
>
> *I raised my eyes. I saw, above me, a judge in a black robe pounding on his desk.*
>
> *"You are charged with false pride, holding yourself above your classmates. You embarrassed friends who trusted you. How do you plead?"*
>
> *"Not guilty," I said, without realizing the words were coming out of my mouth.*
>
> *"The evidence, however, your Honor," the prosecutor, who was standing nearby, protested, "is quite clear. The defendant tried to push ahead, to be first in everything. She bribed her teachers by offering answers to all questions and challenging those of others, preparing reports before they were due and working on every new project. We have witnesses for every event and dates for each exhibit. Do you still plead not guilty?"*
>
> *I was stunned and confused. "I don't remember. I didn't know ..."*
>
> *"Your Honor," the prosecutor continued, "she did know. She violated a law she had just learned: 'You shall not shame your neighbor in public. Rather throw yourself into a burning cauldron first.' Your Honor, she knew, yet chose to reject that knowledge and the severe penalty for*

its disregard."

"How do you plead now? Still innocent?"

"No, no, I'm guilty, guilty," I cried out, *tears dripping down my cheeks.*

"In that case, since this is a first offense, you shall be on probation for the rest of this school year. Go correct your errors."

A funny thing happened to me in the morning. I woke up refreshed and relaxed and full of energy. I've got many exciting things to do. First, I must talk to Savta. I have so much to learn.

XVII
Exciting News

Savta Sadie was sitting in the lounge with her walker beside her. I hugged and kissed her.

"Let's sit here a while and talk. I can't walk too much yet, but I try."

"We can use a wheelchair if you wish."

"I'd rather wait to get stronger by walking than sit in any wheelchair. Once I get in, I won't come out. It's too easy a way to get around."

I was surprised at her strong will.

"Great. Imma loved the tapestry you made. Please, don't try to make any more things until you're all better. I still feel sad about the story you told me last time about losing your baby many years ago."

"Yes," Savta answered, "I had to send her away when she was two years old to keep her safe. I couldn't leave Germany so I gave her to relatives to take with them. I never saw her again. It was a long time ago. I told you that you remind me of her."

"That's funny. I think Imma came from Germany to the United States and lived here with relatives."

"Yes, *einikel*... many babies and children were given up by their parents, with rivers of tears, so they might live. Your mother was one of them. Look how lucky she was. She got a fine, beautiful daughter like you."

I hugged her again. My imagination went wild. I know it's hardly possible. Yet, could it be that we were related? Imma might know.

When a truck finally brought our lift the next day, I was so excited I forgot to ask. It was a large crate with many of the things we needed. Imma was happy to find nothing broken. We could use our Shabbat dishes in time for the High Holidays. Still, our clothes were wrinkled and had the odor of camphor. We had to air them out by placing some of them in the closets and others on the shower curtain bar in the bathroom. I jumped for joy when I found my favorite dolls and books from Israel. Imma kissed the precious notebooks she needed for her research. Her book collection soon covered all the empty book shelves. Now she can work more at home, so I'll see more of her.

I felt good. I could accept invitations to other bat mitzvahs and not be ashamed to show my face with the same party dress. I noticed Imma was checking her own dresses. I guess she needed them for the holidays and who knows what else.

When I almost gave up hope, a letter arrived from Abba. I found it right after school when I opened the mail box with my own key. It was short. He never found time to write much, but it said all I needed to hear:

> *Dear Pussycat (He always called me pussycat because when I was very small I would sit or lie in his lap quietly and he would pat me softly.)*
>
> *I don't know how you guessed but I always said you were a smart girl. I'm flying to New York City right after Succot for a conference. I have to see some people and present a paper. I'll have free time during the day. My company is paying me to go so I'm staying at a fine hotel*

in town. You will love it.

I miss you very much and I'd like to see you then. It won't hurt you to lose a couple of school days. If Imma objects, come early on Sunday morning. I'll send you money for the air fare from Boston and pick you up. You've never been to New York before and I could show you around the city.

I love you, and give my regards to Imma.

Abba.

I flew up the flight of stairs and hammered on the door.

"What's wrong?"

"Terrific news. A letter from Abba. Read it."

I stood there, my chest pounding away and my hands stretched to get the letter back.

Imma showed no signs of joy.

"It's a nice letter. We'll talk more about it when the check comes."

"Imma, how can you be so cold? He's trying to be nice. Couldn't you be at least a little warm about it? He wrote to us."

"He wrote to you. He always tried to get to me through you. I'm willing to wait and see. I never said you can't go. I don't like his remark about taking off time from school."

"All right, but I still feel great."

I kissed the letter and folded it away safely in my jewelry box.

Guess I can't blame Imma. Abba disappointed her many times. But he does want to see me and show me New York. I could soon have new, exciting adventures.

"Imma," I said that evening, "all our things came just in time for the Holidays. Too bad we're going to be all alone. Last year we had lots of friends over and we had our own succah that we had so much fun decorating. What are we going to do this year?"

"It's not that bad. There are many things we can do. We can

invite the Tanarofs whom we haven't seen in a while. They were with us last year in Israel. Some of your nearby classmates might come with their families. I really owe Mr. Miller an invitation. He goes out of his way to be friendly – though I want to be careful with him.

"Don't worry about the succah. You know the synagogue arranges home hospitality. Besides, Dr. Graubard invited us for all the succah meals, if we want to come. Of course, I'll bring along some of the foods you like – and I hope they like them, too."

"Imma," I interrupted, "you know what I want. I like your celery root salad, *gruenkern* soup, and the challah and *schnecken* you bake from your secret recipes. Those would surprise them."

"Yes, if I can find the time. I was going to say I'm sure Yoni will have no objection if you offered to help him decorate their succah."

My eyes popped out. "Really? I can't believe it. That's terrific. You know, we're friendly again in class. He's a big help with my work."

"I didn't know you were unfriendly."

"Anyway, things are shaping up. You mentioned Dr. Graubard. It made me think of his wife and Savta Sadie's child. You know, I was wrong about Savta. She didn't lose a baby. She had to give her own child away when she was two. Relatives brought the baby to America. When I heard this story I thought of you. Could she be my real Savta?"

I looked straight at Imma.

"Not likely. Many parents gave up their young children to relatives in other countries, to Jewish families living among non-Jews, and even to families who were not Jewish, and also to churches. When the few living parents came back, some got their children right away, some couldn't find them. Others had to fight to get them back because some non-Jews wanted to keep them or because some churches claimed they were no longer Jews. I guess Savta Sadie never found her relatives here. She must have had a hard struggle."

"Savta said exactly what you did. Still, we could make-believe she is our Savta. Wouldn't it be great to have her here for the holidays or Shabbat?"

"It certainly would. We could invite her. Make sure you don't get carried away. Why don't you find out her last name."

"That's a great idea. It's just what I'm going to do."

XVIII
HOLIDAY ENJOYMENT

Savta Sadie," I asked on my next visit, "you look much better. Are you ready to take a walk and sit in the garden outside?"

"I still need my walker, but I'd love to go out and sit beside you."

"You see," I pointed out, "the flowers have waited for us and the garden is still full of color, like the tapestry you made for me. I love it."

"Yes, it's so beautiful. And I feel so good to be here with you."

"Savta, could you tell me more about your story? What else do you remember about your little girl?"

"Well, I did get letters for a while, until we were all taken to Auschwitz. I once had pictures of her, all gone now. I never forgot how she looked. I think I said you reminded me of her. That was a long, long time ago," she sighed.

"When I was freed, I came to this country with a friend who had relatives in Indiana. I tried to locate mine but no one knew much about them so many years later. They must have moved. I never found out anything."

"Then you have no family – and we don't, either. I was

wondering, would you be able to come and be with us for Shabbat or holidays?"

"Oh," she squeezed me tight, "I was hoping you might ask, but I never dreamed it would happen. I don't know if I'm strong enough yet. You'd have to ask the chief nurse."

On our way out I stopped at Nurse Rosenthal's office. She was in and ready to talk to me.

"I was wondering if Sadie could come home with us for a weekend or holiday?"

"You mean Savta Sadie?" Nurse Rosenthal was smiling.

"Yes. How did you know?"

"It gets around. People hear things."

"Could she?"

"Right now, she really should not. We want her to regain all her health. You have helped make her stronger. Perhaps later on."

"At Hanukkah time?"

"Perhaps. We shall see. We know we can trust you to care for her needs."

"Could you tell me what her last name is?"

"Since you feel attached to her, Shoshanna, I can tell you that her last name is Steinhaus."

Thank you." I held my breath and tried to smile. I remembered Imma telling me her childhood name was Kornblatt.

"What were you talking to Nurse Rosenthal about?" Jackie asked me on the way home.

"When I saw how lonesome Savta Sadie was, I thought it might be nice to invite her home for a Shabbat or holiday."

"Invite her home?"

"You see," I tried hard to be calm and soft, "Sadie has no family and mine is small. I thought we might be together at our home for a weekend. Nurse Rosenthal said Sadie was too weak to go now."

"I never thought of that," Dalia said. "It might be a good deed to have them see a real home for a change."

When I got home, I told Imma that Savta Sadie's last name was Steinhaus. I felt bad. Imma said she expected it would be different.

"You still wouldn't mind her coming to be with us, would you?"

"Of course not, Shoshi."

"She probably couldn't come before Hanukkah – and that's a long way off."

* * *

Abba's check really came this time.

"See, Imma. He kept his word and even wrote your name on the check."

"So far so good. Let's wait 'til he comes." Imma said, and I said nothing.

Because Rosh Hashanah and Succot came out on weekends and the one free Sunday was hectic, we missed going to the Home for four weeks. I called each week to find out how Savta Sadie was and talked to her on the phone. Strange, I really miss her when I don't visit. I feel she is part of my family.

For Yom Kippur we did something different. Instead of Brookline, we decided to go with the Tanarofs to synagogue services at Rambam School. The hall was full of people, young and old. We had reserved seats to be sure we could rest after our long stroll. I knew most of the boys who were cantors. I thought Yoni might be one of them. He wasn't there.

Imma and Mrs. Tanarof sat together. I took Adele over to my classmates. Donny and Batyah joined the younger children in the larger classrooms.

We enjoyed it all – the chanting, singing, Torah reading – even the *drashas* given by the older boys. At first I wondered if it was OK to enjoy a Day of Atonement. Then I remembered our teacher telling us before the holidays that Yom Kippur is not meant to be a day of sorrow. It was a time for getting clean inside, like a shower to wash away all the dirt we collected over the year, to get rid of all the wrong things we did and to start afresh with good deeds. Fasting, he said, is to remind us that sometimes it is important to do without things, without pleasures. Also, being hungry makes our minds sharper, so we can think clearly and remember what we are doing this day. To tell the truth, fasting all day doesn't bother me. Only at the end before it's dark do I get a headache.

Imma was right about Succot. Dr. Graubard invited only the two of us. Yoni asked me to help with the succah. I decorated it as I did in Israel. I made the egg-shell birds and put streamers across the whole succah. Together we tied strings to apples, carrots, peppers and grapes to beautify the succah with different colors. On the walls we attached large posters of the Old City, of Bible heroes, of succah blessings and our own drawings of "Welcome to our Succah."

It was great to sit inside the succah and look through the green branches covering the top and watch the slow-moving patches of clouds in the open sky. Dr. Graubaud and his sons blended their voices well and we chimed in with them.

Now, I'm sure men can make good meals. Imma helped by adding foods I liked and cakes and kugels. Dr. Graubard did not seem to mind when Imma took charge of the kitchen during the meal.

Yoni's older brother, Menashe, came home from Baltimore for the holidays. He's more serious than Yoni, but easy to talk to. He was eager to learn about Israel because he planned to study in a yeshiva there. I could only tell him about my school. I didn't know much about yeshivas. Maybe he listened to be polite.

One good thing Menashe did do for us. He insisted we go to the Bostoner Rebbe for Simhat Torah, to visit the shul of the Hassidim. That was the place, he said, where on this day everyone gets inspired – shouting, dancing, singing, and everything. Menashe led us on the trail straight along Beacon Street to the shul. I guess he had been there before.

I was surprised how small it was: only a big house and cramped with too many people. Yet, somehow, when the *hakafot* began, space opened up to march around the *bimah* for all who wanted to dance,sing, stamp and pound the floor. The *rebbe*, with his white, full beard, looked old and tired.

Yet, when the dancing and singing started, carrying his small Torah, he was the first to join in, always holding his head high and raising his voice aloud with deep feeling.

Menashe pulled his father and Yoni into the dancing group. They borrowed Torahs from others and circled and swirled about until I got dizzy watching them. The men never seemed to tire. They sang and danced and yet were never out of breath, even though their *kippot* fell off their heads and their shirt tails flapped about.

Sometimes they formed a single line, which became so long they had to go dancing and singing into the nearby street. Everybody outside was watching and enjoying the show of religious feeling and activity. The songs they sang were really verses in the prayer book which came from the Bible. They kept singing them over and over again and never seemed to get tired of repeating the same words.

It was lucky everyone had to get a chance to carry a Torah. Otherwise, the dancing would have gone on forever. After Dr. Graubard and his sons had their *aliyahs*, we all went down to the basement where the women of the shul were serving a luscious *kiddush*. Dr. Graubard said the *kiddush* blessing on the wine as we all sat about a table to enjoy the chicken platters, lukshon kugel, cholent, and the honey and chocolate cakes. I wouldn't be hungry before lunch!

During the long walk back, Dr. Graubard stayed near me while

Imma talked with his two sons. He was very interesting, telling me lots of stories about the many places where he had been. He told me that when he was a youth he fought in Israel's wars and then he traveled to Europe to study. Then he returned to the United States because his whole family was here and got married. I saw that he likes talking, though I wondered why he was telling me all this. I really enjoyed listening to his stories even though I didn't ask him to tell them to me.

After we were together, I thought about him all that day. It was strange that Imma said nothing after we were with them all that time. He seemed to be a very good father. I was impressed with him.

On Tuesday, Imma made a surprise announcement.

"Tomorrow night we're going ice skating at Harvard. It's my late night and I invited Yoni and his father to be our guests at the rink. It's a small return for all they did for us on Succot."

"Imma, that's terrific! I can't wait!"

It was a beautiful rink. Only people connected with Harvard and their guests were allowed to enter. We put on our ice skates and Yoni and I went out on the ice. I had tried ice skating once or twice before in Israel. I saw that Yoni skated well and he showed me how he made figure-eights. But I was clumsy on the ice. Yoni came over and took my arm and slowly we glided along the edge of the rink. It seemed so easy with him. I smiled, looking up into his eyes, and he smiled back.

I didn't see Imma but I figured that she and Dr. Graubard were together somewhere Or maybe they were watching us. I know Imma can skate well. In Israel we took a whole vacation day to enjoy the skating at Bat Yam, where there is an ice rink.

I have a funny feeling calling him Dr.Graubard. It sounds so distant and aloof, especially since Imma calls him by his first name, Yehoshua. I don't know what's appropriate for me.

I love Abba but I think I could learn to like Dr. Graubard a lot.

Thursday night the phone rang. Imma answered.

"Do you want to talk to Shoshi?" She turned to me. "Here, it's Abba."

"Hello, Abba? You're in New York? Great! Yes, I think I can come. I haven't seen you in such a long time! I'll ask Imma. Imma, can I go Sunday morning? Abba said he'll meet me at the LaGuardia airport where the planes come in. Is it all right?"

"All right, you can go. What about coming back?"

"How will I get back, Abba? Oh.....Imma, Abba says he checked and there's no late plane on Sunday night to Boston. He'll take me in very early Monday morning and I'll get to school in time. He'll give me money for a taxi, and I'll only miss services, no classes. OK?"

"Yes, but remember. He must keep his promise about Monday morning."

"OK, Abba, I'm coming."

XIX
DISCOVERING NEW YORK

I thought I'd be scared flying alone and was surprised Imma let me go. I guess she does trust me. Still, she asked the stewardess at the airport to look after me. When we landed I followed the crowd to the luggage room to get my small suitcase. It didn't take long, not like coming from overseas.

I waited outside to watch for Abba. Cars, taxis, and buses were driving up to the curb all the time, dumping out people and their luggage. And, then, right away swallowing up new people and new luggage and speeding away.

"Shoshi."

Abba! I jerked my head towards the voice. There he was, leaning against a small blue car. Dropping my suitcase, I ran to him. He flipped me up in his arms and hugged me tight. I put both my arms around his neck and kissed him.

"You look so grown up I can't believe it, a real beauty," he said.

"You look great too, Abba."

He still had the same big smile and twinkling brown eyes and thin face and deeply sun-tanned skin. I could see his hair was getting grey and he seemed older and weaker. His voice didn't have the power it once had. He was searching for something. I couldn't say what. Was he too much alone?

I know I missed him and was so glad to see him. I always wondered what he was doing. Now he was here with me.

"How was the trip?" he asked.

"Fine."

"Are you glad you're here?"

"Sure. I've been waiting to hug you for centuries."

"I'm happy to hear you say that. I've missed you."

"I love you, Abba." Again, he held me very tight.

"We're going to my hotel in Manhattan later. I'll take you first on a fast tour to some of the sights. We'll have lunch together. In New York you don't have to worry about kosher restaurants. I'm happy you came on Sunday. I have the whole day off."

He was very eager to talk to me and take me places. It all made me feel good. Still a lot of questions popped up in my mind.

"Where did you get this car? It's so pretty and new."

"I rented it. It costs money but saves time. You'll like it because we can go places."

"Where did you get all the money – for the car, my plane trip ...?"

"What's the good of having money if you don't spend it or use it? You're here and we're going to spend some of it on you."

Abba sped ahead to "show you what you never saw before." I felt like I was on a magic carpet tossed about from place to place by a swift wind. Abba wanted to take me everywhere, to see everything. But would I have time to really learn anything?

He drove us to the United Nations Headquarters, showed me the beautiful halls and bought me stamps for my collection. I saw all kinds of tourists and people who work there from all over the world. It was exciting.

After an early lunch at a vegetarian restaurant on 48th street, we were back in the car.

Abba took me all the way down the East River drive. I always read the street signs to know where I was.

"We're passing along the older parts of New York on your right. You can't see much of them. The East Side is where most newcomers first found places to stay and worked very hard to make a living. We are going to pass the famous Wall Street where a good deal of this country's business goes on. Now we are approaching Battery Park where the first Dutch settlers landed. We will park here and meet the world's most famous lady."

"Who's that?"

Abba smiled. "The lady with the torch. The Statue of Liberty."

I had never heard of her before. I could not admit it to Abba. Maybe he knew that, because sometimes he does like to tease. We took the boat ride to Liberty Island and, on the way, Abba pointed to Ellis Island.

"All immigrants had to come here first to see if they could stay in the United States. Millions of people pushed through its gates. Those who were sick or had nowhere to go or no relatives to meet them could be sent back to the countries they fled, even though they came so far and spent all their money to get away from bad conditions and wanted to start a new life in a new country."

On Liberty Island we learned all about how the statue got there, how tall it was, and how many people visit it. I read the words at the bottom of the statue:

"Give me your tired, your poor,

Your huddled masses yearning to breathe free,

The wretched refuse of your teeming shore.

Send these, the homeless, tempest tossed, to me:

I lift my lamp beside the golden door."

I didn't know what all the words meant, but I could feel them. Abba said the poem was written by Emma Lazarus especially for this statue. How different, I thought, these words were from what Abba told me happened on Ellis Island.

"We're turning around and going north on the West Side Highway. If you look on the left, you will see all kinds of ships, maybe a ship from Israel.

"Manhattan is an island, and now we are approaching the middle part of Manhattan where most of the excitement is.

Abba drove us down Forty-Second Street. I never saw that many movie houses. I don't think that Israel has so many. He then turned into Broadway where the cars filled the streets in all directions. The scene reminded me of Jerusalem's busy streets. I was thinking that I don't know how anybody can be safe. Mobs of people were going in and coming out of movie houses, theatres, restaurants and stores that lined the streets.

We drove on and on and finally came close to a park.

"Here's Columbus Circle named for the statue of Columbus in the center. You know he discovered America. We'll drive by Central Park, the one beautiful park in Manhattan, and then go through it. You'll see people running and bicycling up and down the roads. On the other side will be the Metropolitan Museum of Art, one of the most beautiful museums in the world. It has great collections of art treasures from the past and the present. It would take days to see it all, and we don't have the time. Maybe next time."

My eyes were turning this way and that until I got a kink in my neck. So much to see and so little time to see it. But something else bothered me.

"Tour's over. We're going down towards Ramada Inn, our hotel. I booked us there because it's close to Broadway and the restaurants where I eat."

"Abba, I'm puzzled. Why were you taking me on this whole tour?"

He was not sure what to say and hesitated. Then, he looked in my eyes.

"I guess... it was to make you proud of me."

Gently he put his arm about my shoulders. It felt so good to be close.

Abba drove his car into the hotel garage. In his room he put my bag on the bed near the window.

"This is a small hotel compared with others. Still, it's clean and neat and has all I need. After we wash up and rest a bit, we're going to walk down Broadway. You'll be able to say you stepped on the sidewalks of New York."

We started walking on 48th Street. Abba showed me the different stores with all kinds of funny and fancy things like watches, radios, cameras, computers and electrical toys.

Then Abba took me into one of the biggest stores.

"I'm going to buy you something that will be fun and educational at the same time. It's a radio with a recorder. You can listen to music or news, enjoy music on tapes, or make up your own music. You can tape your teacher's speech or lecture or practice your own speeches."

Abba showed me how to put in tapes, record with them and play them. I had seen these recorders before. Now I owned one. I was so happy. Imma would be able to use it, too, to practice the speeches she has to give.

After we left the store, we went past Times Square. It was mobbed with people and cars rushing back and forth. It seemed to me they didn't know where they were going.

"Look up," Abba said. "Watch the news of the world move before you in bright lights."

There it was near the top of a building. Hundreds of electric bulbs were blinking out messages in words that seemed to move across and then disappear. It was like watching something magical.

"Now, we're going to an unusual place for dinner. It's a kosher Chinese restaurant called Moshe Peking. You'll love it. Everything will be very different and tasty."

When we got there, Abba suggested I order a pepper steak, which I tried to eat by picking up rice and pieces of meat with chopsticks. Soon I gave up and asked for a fork. It was much easier to use and I then really enjoyed the dish.

After the restaurant, we went to see a Walt Disney movie.

It was about real families and full of fun. By the time we got back to the hotel, I was exhausted, but I saw Abba wanted to say something.

"I'd like to talk to you. I see you're sleepy but I hope you don't mind if I ask you one question. Do you really have to go back so soon tomorrow morning? We haven't been together in a whole half-year. We should have time for at least one good talk."

"I'd like to talk to you too, but I must go back tomorrow to school."

"Would you miss school?"

I laughed.

"I have a busy schedule at school, the honors program. If I miss a day, I have to make up the work. But," I smiled at Abba, "I guess one day wouldn't hurt too much. I could handle it. Maybe we'll find some time to talk early in the morning."

"Good night, then, and sweet dreams. More adventures tomorrow."

XX
AN ALMOST TRAGIC ACCIDENT

At first I fell fast asleep, but later during the night I became restless. I couldn't figure out what was bothering me. Why was Abba so nice all day? Spending so much money? No, it's something else. What was it I didn't do? There was something I forgot to do yesterday, on Sunday?

Too late I remembered. In my excitement to see Abba I forgot all about Savta Sadie. Imma did not remind me. Of course, it wasn't her job. It was mine. At least I should have called her when I knew I was not coming. I don't know how she is. She may worry about me for nothing. I should call her. I hope Savta Sadie doesn't get sick again. I began to feel sad and guilty.

Wait! Another thing! I promised Imma that I would come home early.

But I have a right to be here. It's my Abba. He has a right to talk to me. But Imma is right, too. I shouldn't miss school.

That night I kept twisting and turning from side to side. I did not know which was the right thing to do. I was too awake to rest or to dream and too sleepy to awaken.

When I did open my eyes it was daytime.

"What happened? Abba, where are you?"

"Right here. You looked so tired I thought it was a sin to shake you. I touched you gently but you didn't waken."

"Our plane? When do we go? I must rush!"

"It's too late. Call your mother and tell her what happened. That's best. You'd miss half the school day anyway if you went now."

"Where's the phone?" I was very scared and felt my head pound. I dialed our apartment.

"Imma?"

"Yes, where are you?"

"In New York."

"What happened?"

"I overslept."

"Why didn't Abba wake you."

"I guess I was too tired out to wake up. We did so much yesterday. Please call the school and tell them the story."

"No, you promised to be back early. Both of you gave your word."

"But, Imma, we couldn't help it."

"Everybody can help it. You just have to want to and your father just doesn't want to."

"Please, Imma. Just this one time?"

"Only if you promise to be back as soon as you can this very day."

"I promise."

"All right. I'll get your homework for tomorrow."

"Thanks. I knew I could depend on you. Could you call Savta? She might worry about me."

"I already did, early Sunday morning."

"Thanks again, Imma." Then, I turned to Abba.

"Wow, I'm so glad that's over. I wouldn't know what to do without Imma. You must find another flight to take me back to Boston," I told Abba.

"Who is this Savta?"

"Oh, she's an old woman I take care of at the Home."

"Shoshi, this may be all for the best. Now we have our chance to talk."

"Not now, please. We could talk on the way back to the airport."

"This I must tell you now. I have a good job and a nice apartment in Yerushalayim. But I'm all alone most of the time. Then I realized you must be lonesome away from all your friends there, especially Dvorah. So I thought maybe you'd like to have a short trip to see them all. Only for a week. I have to leave tomorrow morning and we could go together. I'd buy you tickets to go there and return. What do you think of that?"

"To Israel? To see Dvorah? Do you see that I wear my half of the *Mizpah* charm? She wears the other half. I wrote to her, but she did not answer yet."

"Just for one week, that's all. Don't worry about any clothes. I'll buy you what you need."

"You mean it? To Jerusalem?" My heart jumped. My hand reached up to touch my necklace.

"Yes."

"What about Imma and school?"

"You know you can easily make up one week's work. You've been with Imma all the time. Why can't you be with me for a short while? That's all I ask."

"Then I must call her right away."

I rang again; the line was busy. I waited and rang again. Still busy.

The third time, Imma answered.

"Imma, how did it go?"

"Why the question? You know I'd do whatever you asked. Why aren't you on your way to the airport?"

"We haven't found the right flight yet. Something new has also come up."

"What do you mean?"

"Abba wants me to go to Jerusalem with him for one week to see my friends."

"No, absolutely no. I knew I could not trust him to see you."

"Oh, Imma, why must you talk like that? Why can't you trust him this time? I've been with you all the time. He only wants one week. He's going to pay for my plane tickets and buy me clothes there. I won't miss the schoolwork. I can make it up with no trouble. You know that."

"*NO, NO, NO!* You can't go. I want you back here immediately! There's no other choice."

"Imma, only for one week."

"*NO, NO, NO!*"

"I only want to see my friends. I miss them."

"Shoshi, you are driving me out of my mind. Where are you now?"

"At the Ramada Inn."

"Stay right there! I'm going to come and get you."

I heard her slam the phone down.

"What happened?" Abba asked.

"Imma wants to come and get me."

"We'll see. I have a meeting this morning. Then I'll get your flight tickets. Wait here. I won't be too long."

I was all mixed up. Abba was very good to me. I had lived with Imma and not with him for years. Why would one week do so much harm? Still, we had both promised Imma. I should keep my word. I didn't know what to do.

After that argument with Imma, I had to lie down and rest my tired, troubled brain. I closed my eyes.

The phone rang loud. I jumped up, shaken, and grabbed the ear piece.

"Hello, who is this?"

"This is the Community Hospital calling. Is this Shoshanna Bernstein?"

"Yes."

"Your mother asked us to call. She had a minor accident."

"An accident? My mother?"

"Yes, she keeps asking for you."

"Are you sure? Let me talk to her?"

"She's sleeping now. We gave her a sedative to ease her pain."

"Oh, no, it can't be? Where are you?"

"200 Brookline Avenue. She's in Room 208."

"I'll get there right away."

The tears started rolling down my cheeks. It can't be. My Imma never gets sick or hurt. Something terrible must have happened.

Just then Abba walked in with tickets in his hands.

"I can't go. Imma's in the hospital; she's hurt," I cried bitterly.

XXI
SLOW RECOVERY

I couldn't control myself and wasn't ashamed. I cried so bitterly on my flight to Boston I thought my heart would break. The people around me must have thought I was crazy.

It's my fault. Imma is the best in the whole world. Because of me she got hurt and might die! Why did I do it? How could I be so selfish?

I hope, I just hope, she's all right. She must be. I could not live without her. She's all I have. I must get there fast.

The stewardess came over a few times to ask what was wrong.

I couldn't tell her. I said, "Nothing." I guess she didn't believe me. I was not ready to share.

As I was getting off the plane my eyes were so full of tears that I couldn't see my way. A lady next to me offered tissues and put her arm around my shoulder.

"What's wrong, my child?" I looked up. She seemed to have a kind face.

"My mom's in the hospital. She had an accident. I have to get to her."

"Oh, I'm so sorry. Would you like me to take you there?"

"I was told not to go with strangers. Thank you just the same."

The stewardess heard us talk as we passed by the plane door.

"You can trust Mrs. Johnson. I know her well. She's with the police."

"Oh, then could you help me? It's the Einstein Medical Center. I must get there as soon as I can."

Abba had actually given me money for a taxi to the hospital but I was afraid to go alone. Mrs. Johnson drove me in her car. I tried to explain a little about why I was out of school and visiting my father in New York. Maybe I shouldn't have said anything. I didn't tell her the reason for the accident or that my parents were divorced.

My new friend was able to get me to Room 208 right away. The nurse asked me to be quiet since Imma was asleep. She looked worn out and weak. Long plastic tubes, like crawling, choking snakes, were circling about and coming out of her. I felt so guilty. My eyes started to fill with tears again. I tiptoed to the side of her bed and put her hand in mine. I touched her face gently.

Poor Imma. All this happened to her because she loved me and worried about me. Why was she punished when I was to blame?

Mrs. Johnson had to leave.

"Don't forget. If you need any help, please call me. Here's my card."

"Thank you for bringing me." I shook her hand good-bye.

I sat in a seat near the bed, waiting and hoping. I heard Imma sigh deeply and slowly open her eyes.

"Imma," I began to cry and smile at the same time, "I'm sorry about what I did. I'm sorry it ever happened."

"Shoshi, my child," Imma said, "you're here! Thank God. That's all that matters. I thought I would never see you again."

"Oh, no, I would NEVER do that, Imma."

"I didn't know what to think. I was so confused. I ran out looking for a taxi to take me to the airport."

She spoke very slowly like she was having trouble finding the right words.

"That's when it happened?"

"Yes, I ran into the street to hail a cab. Next thing I knew I was in this bed."

"Imma, are you badly hurt?"

"They're not sure yet. They're taking X-rays to see if any bones are broken. I had a bad headache which is beginning to clear up. I don't think it's serious... I don't know."

"I'm worried about you."

"I know how you feel. Don't worry. Everything will turn out all right."

"How long will you be here?"

"I don't know," she smiled. "Let's wait 'til the doctors finish their tests."

The door to mother's room swung open. Dr. Graubard rushed in. His face was white as chalk and knotted up like he was in pain. Imma held out her right arm to him. He reached the opposite side of the bed and gripped her hand tightly. He was nervous as he spoke and took rapid breaths.

"Tova, the call just came from the hospital. I left immediately. I'm relieved to find you awake and alert."

Here I was sitting right across from him and Dr. Graubard didn't see me or say hello.

Last time he was very friendly. It's the first time I ever heard him call Imma by her first name. What did it all mean?

He talked to Imma a long time before he turned around toward me.

"Shoshanna, it's good to see you. You're always the dependable daughter."

Didn't he know anything about what happened to me? Imma didn't tell him?

"Your mother may have to be here a while. Would you like to stay with us?"

For a moment my heart leaped. Then, I changed my mind.

"No, I can't. Thanks. My books and school things and clothes are at home. My friends will call me. I know where everything is and I can make my own meals. My car pool picks me up there. I'll be OK, really."

They were not the true reasons. I didn't like what Dr. Graubard was doing. He was pushing me away and taking my Imma from me. First, I thought it would be great for Imma to have a friend so she wouldn't be lonely. I worked hard to find someone. Now I'm not so sure. I love Imma and no one is going to take her from me. I was getting angrier and angrier.

"Imma," I burst out, "I'm going to come here every morning and stay with you. I can help you so you'll have somebody near you all the time."

"The nurses take very good care of me."

"They come and go and I'll be with you always."

"Shoshi, you can't. I don't think they allow it. Besides, you have to go to school."

"You're more important than my school work. Life comes before study."

"I know, but there's nothing you can do here."

"I'm coming. I'll be with you all the time."

I spoke real loud. Imma became very irritated.

"There's very little you can do here. The nurses come when I need them. I press this button to send for them. They know exactly what to do for me. Sometimes I want to rest and sleep."

"Your mother's right," Dr. Graubard added. "Let's not distress her. You can't stay away from school like that. We understand your good intentions but learning is very important."

I didn't ask him to tell me. I know school's important. And I'm not his daughter. Imma comes first, especially when I need her. She's all I have and he wants to take her away. I wasn't distressing her; he was.

I think I'll find a flight to take both of us far away where nobody can mix in our family. Maybe we can go back to Israel and my friends, after all.

"Would you come to us for Shabbat?"

I jerked up my head to look at him. "Maybe." I guess I didn't mean it. My jaws were so tight my teeth hurt.

On the way home Dr. Graubard wanted to talk. I was not in the mood and remained silent.

When I got home, I could see that Imma left in a hurry. The house was a big mess, with things all in disarray. I straightened it all out as best I could, ate an afternoon snack, and then sat down to do the studying I missed on Sunday.

The calls began, one after another: Dalia, Andrea, Jackie, Gabby, Mindy, and some of my teachers.

They're all great, really friends in need and the teachers, too. They wanted to help me and have me stay with them. I couldn't tell them everything. They knew I was in New York on Sunday because I had missed the visit to the Residential Home. I said nothing about the Israel trip or why Imma got hurt. It wasn't that I was lying; I was not telling. Not even a white lie. Imma didn't tell anyone either. She might be ashamed.

The bell rang. A messenger with a large basket of fruit was at the door.

The card read: "From your friends at Harvard."

The phone rang again. It was Dr. Graubard.

"Would you like to go with me to see your mother this evening?

If you can spare time from your studies, I know she'd love to see you."

"Thanks, Abba – I mean Dr. Graubard. I'm sure I can spare the time."

I was shocked. He wants me to see Imma, not to take her from me! And why did I say Abba?

"Oh, a basket of fruit came from Harvard. Should we take it?"

"I think so. Your mother might like to see it."

That evening mother looked more awake and stronger. I came in holding the basket high.

"What's that?" she asked

"From your friends at Harvard."

"I can't eat all that."

"Fruit is healthy; it's good for you."

"They feed me very well. I guess we can all enjoy it. Some good news. The X-rays showed no broken bones. The doctor said I had strained tendons and wrenched muscles that need time to heal. My head's all clear. The CAT scan – the pictures of my brain – showed nothing wrong."

I was very relieved to hear this, and so was Dr. Graubard. I was surprised he let me talk and didn't say anything, only listened and smiled.

He took me to see Imma every evening for a whole week. We enjoyed talking on the rides. He wasn't a bad person. It was easy to like him. But I was very worried about Imma. When would she ever be released from the hospital?

XXII
OLD-NEW MEMORIES

Imma came home after ten days in the hospital. She was on crutches but soon didn't need them. Her legs and right arm hurt. She didn't complain. Dr. Graubard drove her to Harvard to teach classes. The rest of the time she worked at home. Now I didn't mind him taking her. He was only trying to help.

What got me worried was the poor shape of my school work. At first, I had to visit Imma at the hospital. Then, after she came home, I had to help her with the cleaning and cooking and everything. I couldn't let her stand on her feet.

I'm not complaining, though I didn`t have much time left. I barely passed my history and Talmud tests and couldn't finish my book reviews on time. It got me down a lot. I knew I needed to find time to catch up when Imma got better.

I couldn't give up the time I visited with Savta. When we got together, I explained to her about my Sunday visit to Abba and about Imma`s accident. She felt very bad for me.

"How do you manage? Don't you need help?"

"Dr. Graubard helps a lot. He's nice... he drives Imma to work and does other things like helping with some of our shopping."

"It's good to have people who want to help."

"He invited us to eat in his succah all week long. Remember, I told you about his son, Yoni, who works with me in science? I helped decorate their succah. I missed not having my own."

"You're such a lovely child. I'm sure he must be a fine boy, too." "He is. Imma helped out, too. She brought her own special foods for the succah meals. He made gruenkern soup, celery root salad and baked challah and *schnecken*. I love them. Have you heard of them?"

"Of course. Your family must come from Germany, too. We made all those foods. And the bread we made was very plain and healthy: no eggs or sugar and very little salt – just water, yeast and flour."

"Imma told me her *schnecken* came from a secret family recipe and so did the challah. She learned it all from her aunt."

"Secret recipes? I think every family has their own secret recipes. My sister and I got our recipe because our mother cooked with us."

"Really? Funny, the more we talk the closer we get – in everything."

"We're close enough already. I love you just as you are. I was wondering why didn't her mother teach her?"

"Her mother could not come here. Her aunt and uncle raised her in the United States from the time she was a baby."

"That's not new," she laughed. "I gave my little girl to my sister when she left for America. It happened to many people. We talked about it."

Maybe it did happen to many people. Still, I'm getting closer. Anything is possible, and I'm going to work on it. I decided to be my own detective.

First, I searched. I tried to find out where Imma kept her secret recipes. Then, I tried to find where Imma kept her wallet with a picture of herself. I wasn't going to steal them. I was only going to borrow them to show Savta. But I failed in my search; I found nothing. I couldn't do any more on my own. I had to ask Imma.

"Imma, could you help me? I wonder if I could look at your secret recipes and the picture you once showed me. I'd like to know more."

Imma laughed. I love my mother's laugh. It's so real.

"I don't have those recipes written down. They're all in my head. The picture I showed you is still in my wallet."

"Could you write them down? The challah and the *schnecken*? And could you show me the picture, please."

Imma took a sheet from her pad and wrote down two recipes. She opened up her wallet and took out the black and white photo of a little girl.

I smiled and said, "Imma, you look like me when you were young! My baby picture looks like this."

"Yes, I suppose I did. I don't often look at it. You know most little girls seem very much alike, with their round faces, curled hair, big smile and open bright eyes, especially in black-and-white." She laughed again.

"Imma, could I borrow them?"

"I guess you want to show them to Savta Sadie."

"Yes. I'll tell you what I'm going to do. Savta Sadie told me she had secret recipes for bread and *schnecken*. I want to see if they match. Then, I'll show her the picture. You don't mind, do you?"

Sunday was supposed to be our last visit to the Residential Home. I had one more to go because I missed one visit. And I still had to finish my search for a long-lost relative.

Savta and I had to be alone when I showed her what I brought, no matter what happened. I led her to a corner of the garden we liked to sit in together. .

I was so jumpy when I pulled the two recipes out of my pocket to show Savta, I almost tore them in half.

"Savta, would you look at these two papers with the two "secret" recipes?"

Savta straightened and smoothed out the sheets and took them into her thin, bony hands. She read slowly. Her hands began to shake.

"Can't be! They are the exact ingredients my mother used to make *schnecken* and the same way she prepared and rolled the dough... and the way she made the pure challah without eggs or sugar at all. Where did you get these?"

"My mother wrote them down for me."

"And from memory yet. Hard to believe someone else did it the same way."

While she was wondering, I carefully took out the picture and showed it to Savta. She began to cry.

"Where did you get this? It looks just like the ones I lost when I went to Auschwitz. Where did you find them?"

It was good we were alone. Savta kept wiping her eyes and staring at the picture.

"Can't be. It looks so much like a picture I once had. It was so long ago. Maybe I don't remember."

I hugged and kissed Savta Sadie. I was very puzzled, too. Much was the same. Yet we could not be sure. Imma told me pretty girls look alike when they are young. Why should a certain recipe be known only to three or four people in the whole world? My job was not finished. I did not know where to turn or what to do now. I must talk to Imma. I couldn't think about this for long. It was our farewell day and I had to go to the ceremony that they were doing, to give us our certificates. They were going to let me get my certificate with the others since I promised to come back next week.

The whole staff took off fifteen minutes to honor us. They let our own residents stay after the show to watch. We were pinning on the yellow tea roses they gave us at the doorway of the auditorium. While we were waiting, Andrea spoke up.

"You know, guys, I'm going to miss this place. How do you feel about coming back... you know," she said, looking around, "just because we want to?"

"I'd love to," I said, surprised to hear Andrea speak like that, and jumped for joy.

"I'm for it," Jackie added. "It's been a great experience. I've never felt so good helping others like I did here."

"My mom won't mind my coming," Gabby said. "She'd rather have me here than running around."

"OK, guys," Dalia said, "then let's march up on the stage to the tune of 'Rambam-bam-bam-bam, Rambam-bam-bam-bam,' our `new' school marching song. It has a good drum beat." And she drummed away with her knuckles on the nearby wooden door.

We all laughed and picked up her beat as we tapped with our feet on our single-file walk to the front of the auditorium.

On the stage we sat down in a row of chairs next to Nurse Rosenthal. At the podium Dr. Moniker, the administrator, said a few words to introduce Head Nurse Rosenthal.

Then, Mrs. Rosenthal said, "Let me tell everyone what you all did and how much happiness you brought to our Home. We will be very sorry to see you go. I'm going to miss each and every one of you. Please don't forget us."

All of us looked at each other and grinned when we heard her words.

As she called our names, we approached the front of the stage to shake her hand and receive our certificates. When we had all gone back to our places, she turned to us and asked, "Would any of you like to make any comments before we say good-bye?

That was our signal. We all stood up. Jackie, like the foreman of a jury, stepped up to the mike and spoke.

"We all enjoyed spending our time here so much," she paused and looked over the whole room," that we plan to keep coming. So, there's no good-bye!"

For a moment, everyone in the room was still. Then, suddenly, a loud clapping of hands burst forth from the staff and we heard "hurray's" from the residents. I never felt happier in my life.

XXIII
I Solve the Mystery

I mma, I feel like a detective who is solving a mystery. I've got most of the clues except the important ones."

"What do you mean?"

"Remember the gold chain with the Magen David you bought me in Israel? I used to wear it all the time. One day it broke and I lost some links. I looked and never found the missing links and I cried so much. It's the same thing here. I'm looking for the last missing links and I can't find them.

"Many things about Savta Sadie fit our real Savta. Like you said, they could happen to lots of people. We've got to find some facts that don't fit others, only our Savta. I don't know what they are. Do you have any ideas?"

"I really don't. There's nothing more you can do. Besides, you need all your time for school work. I know how much you help me, and you do visit Savta Sadie every Sunday."

It wasn't enough for me. I had to find out more, to know for sure, one way or the other. I said nothing further about my plans to Imma.

"OK, Imma. You know it's getting closer to Hanukkah. I'm sure

Savta Sadie can come. Remember we promised her."

"Of course, she can come. I'd love to see her. I invited Dr. Graubard and his sons. We'll have real family dinners during Hanukkah."

"Imma, why does he call you by your first name?"

"I call him by his first name, too. We're just friendly."

"Imma," I teased – or maybe I wasn't – "are you going to marry him? Is that why you said 'family dinners'?"

"No!" She spoke so strongly. "That's not the reason."

"Well, maybe he's in love with you?"

"Why do you say that?" I thought I saw Imma's cheeks turn red.

"The way he looked when he came to the hospital and the way he held your hand tight… and always agreeing with you and doing things for you."

Imma laughed.

"I guess he likes me, but he never asked me to marry him."

"Could he be thinking about it, Imma?"

"You'll have to ask him."

* * *

All the way to the Resident Home I tried and tried to think of some way to solve my mystery. How could I decide once and for all if Savta Sadie was my real Savta? She says it doesn't matter and she's right. Maybe I should forget about it. That's what Imma says.

When I got there, I saw her waiting for me and felt so close, I changed my mind. Something deep must be there. There was only one way to find out. I must learn more about Savta Sadie's life. Not like a detective or a lawyer asking sharp questions of a witness, but like a listening friend. After all, she's my only witness to her story. She will know the truth.

It was cooler that day. I wrapped Savta in the belted light gray wool coat I found in her closet. Again we walked into the garden to the corner with the four-foot hedge that surrounded the flower garden of red, white and yellow chrysanthemums. "Savta Sadie," I said as we sat down, "I would like to know more about you, to feel closer. Especially about your early life as a child, growing up, getting married and having a baby...."

"I'm happy to tell you. We lived in a small, clean, beautiful town with trees lining the sides of the streets and flower gardens like these planted here. We were two older sisters and four younger brothers. I, the oldest, helped with the other children. I didn't like washing their hands and faces and clothing, but I loved to be in the kitchen, especially for baking. That's where my sister and I learned the recipes."

She stopped for a minute. I thought she was out-of-breath again. This time Savta Sadie was only thinking, remembering.

"I married young and two years later had a beautiful child. My husband became ill and I knew the Nazis would find us. So I had to give our baby away to save her. I couldn't leave my husband. Soon we were taken away. My husband died at the camp. I was strong and lived.

"How we all suffered and starved and froze and slaved and passed away – not pretty stories for your ears or eyes, my angel. I tried to help others want to live when they had nothing worth living for. But enough of that."

"I bet you saved many lives, Savta."

"I hope so. Anyway, one woman had relatives in America who sent for her, after we were out of the camp. She wanted me to go with her. I had no one. So we came to Indiana to live with her relatives, an older brother and sister-in-law.

"Once we were settled, she wanted to help me find my relatives.

We traveled to Springfield, Ohio where my sister once lived, but no one was there. We asked neighbors, the people in the post office and the city hall people. Finally we found out that they had moved long ago to Chicago.

"I went by myself to Chicago. I searched all over. That's how I learned the language, looking in city records, directories, telephone books… and finally, after many years, I gave up the search.. Could be they died, left the city or changed their name to make it more American. I don't know which.

"Here I was, without any family of my own, in Chicago, staying with other relatives of my friend. A cousin of hers wanted to marry me. I agreed because I was getting older. We never had any children, perhaps because of my camp experience. We worked hard together and had a happy life. He was a fine man and truly loved me."

My eyes were popping. I was almost touching the missing link. I recalled that Imma's aunt and uncle once lived in Chicago. Still I was not ready to ask the final questions.

"Savta, how did you get to Boston? It's a long way from Chicago."

"My friend and I kept writing and calling each other, sometimes visiting. As it happened, her older brother and sister-in-law died. Their son, her nephew, offered her their home in Boston. They were all fine people. So she came here. When my husband died, she wanted me to join her.

"I told her it wasn't fair for young people to care for two old women. So her nephew looked around and found this place. We were like sisters here and had a wonderful time. She was older than me and died just a short time ago. I felt all alone again. You came in time to make me feel better. Here it's like Paradise, but even in Paradise you need someone. I have you."

Savta Sadie was finishing telling me her life story. As she kept talking, my heart began to pound stronger and louder, like it was going to beat through the roof of my head. I thought I would burst but I didn't. I kept myself bottled up. I still wasn't sure; I had to be patient. She had to give me the missing clue of my mystery.

"Savta Sadie, then you were married twice?"

"Of course."

"And you had two different last names?"

"Yes."

"What were they?"

"My last name now is Steinhaus and my first husband's family name was Kornblatt. Both good German names."

I thought the glaring light from my wide-open, staring eyes would blind Savta Sadie. My investigation was complete. I could say nothing to Savta then. I just hugged and kissed her so many times, she became very puzzled.

"What is it, my child?"

"As you told me your story, I lived through it with you. I felt part of you, as close as any grandchild can be. Also, Hanukkah is coming soon. Nurse Rosenthal said you could come and be with us during Hanukkah. Promise to come."

"That would be my greatest wish. To be in a fine, warm, happy home and see a real Hanukkah family celebration."

Finally, I had solved my mystery and discovered the truth. I must keep it safe and secret for now. I made my plans. No one would know until I was ready.

XXIV
FOUND: A REAL GRANDMOTHER

Things were happening fast and, yet, slowing down to the way they were before. Imma was almost all better and feeling fine. Dr. Graubard was not visiting so much. Instead he was calling more. I had more time to do my homework and study. I was doing better in school and happier.

What made me feel best was solving our family mystery. I had the secret answer of the life-story of Savta Sadie. Just like in detective stories, everybody involved would find out about it at the same time.

During the week before Hanukkah, I had other surprises. Letters came one after another from my friends in Yerushalayim. Dvorah wrote the most of all, a four-page letter. She told how she cried over my letter and missed me. She wore her *Mizpah* chain, too. As usual, she wrote, the days were very hot, but the nights were cool and refreshing.

She wrote that on Yom Kippur a strong *hamsin* swept in from the east and some people collapsed in synagogues from the heat. She also wrote that school was still the same. She mentioned some of the teachers I liked who sent their regards.

I enjoyed her stories about the girls and boys we both knew

well. And Dvorah didn't forget to send me copies of the photos we took at my farewell party. Again I saw and stared long at the large cake Ednah and her mother baked for me with the words "Shalom Yerushalayim, Shalom Boston" in pink icing. I knew that I had to write back and thank her and the other girls, as soon as I could.

A letter from Abba came unexpectedly a day before Hanukkah. It was short and had a $500 check inside:

> *Dear Pussycat,*
>
> *I hope everything is back to normal in your home. Sorry I didn't write you before. I'm very busy running around and don't find much time to stay in one place. You're probably better off with Imma. With me you'd be alone a good part of the time. She has always taken good care of you.*
>
> *I'm sending you a gift now because I thought you could use it for Hanukkah and for your coming bat mitzvah.*
>
> *All the best and all my love,*
>
> *Abba.*

"Imma, did you see the letter from Abba? There's a $500 check with it. Is he trying to help us?"

"Do you know what it really means?"

"No."

"It's the same money he put away to pay for your one-way flight to Israel, to take you from me."

"Why do you say that? It has your name on it, though it's supposed to be for me."

"When you live with someone long enough, you learn a lot about them. Perhaps he's come to his senses. Instead of taking you away from me, he's sending money to help you stay with me. He thought it over and realized it would be a mistake to take you there. He feels bad about what he planned to do. Once in a while he can do the right thing, though he can't admit it."

"You noticed he said nothing about my accident."

"Yes, Imma, that was funny."

"That's because Abba doesn't like to face problems. He just wants to be happy and do what he likes. If he could take you to Israel and show you around, that would be fun. Taking care of you and your needs every day of the year would be too much for him.

"You know, I don't hate him. I feel sorry for him, but I don't want him for a burden over my head."

I was beginning to understand Abba and, like Imma, felt sorry for him.

Finally, the afternoon of the fifth day of Hanukkah arrived. This was the big day I planned to bring Savta Sadie to our home. We would all be together to light the candles for the sixth night.

Dr. Graubard drove me to the Home and we picked her up.

She was dressed in a pretty blue dress I had never seen before. She seemed to be glowing.

"Good-bye, folks," she called, "I'm going to visit my family for Hanukkah."

It all worked out beautifully. Dr. Graubard chanted the blessings over the *Hanukkiah*, our Hanukkah menorah. He lighted one candle, gave the *shammash* to Imma, who passed it to Menashe, to Yoni and finally to me, each of us lighting one candle in turn. I gave it to Savta whose face was simply beaming. Her hands were stronger than I ever saw them. She lighted the sixth candle on her first try.

We all clapped our hands and sang "These Lights" and "Rock of Ages" in Hebrew as Savta listened and looked at us all, turning from one to the other.

We had a delicious meal with lots of joking and laughing. For our dessert, we served homemade latkes and applesauce, the ones that I had I helped Imma prepare. Everyone except Savta took part in the cleanup.

"You are the guest of honor," I told her and she smiled. Then Imma and Dr. Graubard covered the dining room table with Hanukkah gifts. As they were about to give them out, I stopped them. I was going to be in charge, like a conductor leading an orchestra.

"We've talked about the story of Hanukkah and what it means and how it's a time for dedication and learning about heroes and martyrs. Now I want you all to hear a different story which tells about dedication, heroes and martyrs.

"Savta Sadie, would you tell us about your life – like you told me, so everyone will hear it?" I asked with pleading eyes.

Savta started to talk, in her pleasant voice, telling her moving history. Only Imma would know whose story this was supposed to be. I watched my mother carefully. I thought I saw her wince as if in pain and catch her breath every time she heard words, names or stories she might have remembered, like "husband was ill," "sister with two-year-old baby," "Auschwitz," "came to America," "Springfield, Ohio," and "Chicago." Her face was turning paler and paler as she stared at Savta Sadie. Finally, Savta finished with her arrival at Boston to be with her friend and settling in the Residential Home.

Now I began to ask her a few questions, as I did when we were alone.

"Savta Sadie, you were married twice?"

"Yes, I told you. You know that."

"I wanted to make sure. Then you must have had two last names?"

"Of course. My last name now is Steinhaus. The family name of my first husband was "Kornblatt."

Imma gasped.

"Oh my God," she shouted and collapsed into a chair. Dr. Graubard rushed to her side, very distressed.

"What's wrong?"

Savta Sadie was disturbed.

"What did I do?"

"Nothing wrong, Savta," I said quietly. "I want you to try to be very calm. You may feel a small shock, but it will be all right. Are you ready?"

"Yes, but what is it?"

"Could you guess why I asked you to tell your whole story?"

"You mean...but it can't be! Are you trying to tell me I'm really your Savta?

"And Mrs. Bernstein..." She turned to look at Imma. "...Is really...really..."-

Imma suddenly stood up, ran over and hugged Savta and cried and cried and cried – "...my own daughter?"

"Yes, yes, your own Tova," my mother said.

Savta's arms trembled as she wrapped them around Imma and joined the flood of tears.

EPILOGUE

We wanted Savta to move in with us. She hesitated. Savta did not want to be a burden to others at this time, especially in a small apartment.

"Later on, we'll see. I like the beautiful garden where I can walk and talk to Shoshi

She laughed and I saw her wink at Imma.

I must admit Imma fooled me – well, actually disappointed me. I was expecting her to say something on the last day of Hanukkah when both families were together. I was sure she was going to make some kind of announcement as she sat opposite Dr. Graubard who was at the head of the table. But she didn't. Is she playing cat-and-mouse games with Dr. Graubard? Or maybe she isn't, or both?

Maybe they aren't ready to get married. At least Imma can't complain about being all alone any more. Anyway, when the time comes, I'm all for it. I'll be getting two grown-up brothers. They can be a great help and I won't have to worry about washing their hands and faces and clothes like Savta had to. I hope they don't set the wedding date close to my bat mitzvah. It's better to have big celebrations a little apart.

Only I have a couple of problems. What should I call Dr. Graubard after Imma marries him? Should I change my last name? If I did, everyone would have the same last name.

I love Abba, but I think I could find room in my heart for Dr. Graubard. It would be more like a regular family. Would Abba think I was not respecting him? I don't know. Of course, I will always be called Shoshanna bat Yeruham. That never changes.

Imma and I are beginning to plan my bat mitzvah celebration. It will be great, especially since Abba's Hanukkah gelt will help. I'm inviting everyone – all my friends, my teachers, and the neighbors I know. Of course, I'll invite Abba. I don't know if he'll come. And I'll send invitations to all my friends in Israel. If they want to come, I'll even make room in our apartment. Imma won't mind. We can always use sleeping bags like we did on our camping trips in Israel. So, at my bat mitzvah I may have a complete family again, including a Savta I never had before. I'm happy that she's happy and healthy because she's always lots of fun to be with, for many years ahead.

And you'll never guess! I just heard some exciting news. Dr. Graubard has been offered a job as professor at the Hebrew University for next year. He's thinking it over. That would be the greatest!

If it happened maybe we could all go to Israel, including Savta. I love and miss Yerushalayim, -and I love and miss my friends there, too.

Actually, I can't wait too long to go back, because I must take Savta with me to show her all of Yerushalayim and

Eretz Yisrael while she can still go about with me on her own. And my friends from Rambam could visit me there.

So, shalom, Jerusalem, l'hitraot, and shalom, Boston, how good to be with you.

GLOSSARY

Abba: Dad, Father

agorah: ancient, small coin; today's value: 100 *agorot* = 1 shekel

aliyah: going up: to Israel as new immigrant or to the Torah reading

balebusteh: a competent woman, particularly in household matters

bat: daughter (of)

bat mitzvah: literally, "daughter of commandments," age at which a girl takes personal responsibility for her actions

brachah: blessing

bimah: platform supporting table upon which the opened Torah scroll is read

Bnei Akiva: religious youth group

(t)cholent: a food cooked slowly for the Sabbath usually containing beans, barley, meat and potatoes

drashas: brief talks explaining Biblical passages

einikel: granddaughter (-son)

Eretz: Land (of)

gelt: money, coins, usually as gifts for Hanukkah

gruenkern: kernels of grains, usually ground

hakafot: circles danced around the *bimah* during Simchat Torah

(c)hallah: bread, usually plaited, normally used on Sabbath and holidays

hamsin: hot, dry eastern wind

Hanukkah: Festival of lights or dedication of the Temple in Jerusalem, celebrating the victories of the Maccabees over Antiochus, Seleucid king of Syria

hanukkiah: eight-branched candelabrum, reminiscent of the menorah in the Temple, lighted for eight days, one candle added each day (also see *menorah*)

(c)hassidim: religious Jews who emphasize joy and spiritual zeal in their daily observances

havdalah: ceremony at the end of a Sabbath or holiday

Hillel House: Jewish student house on a college campus

Imma: Momma, mommy, Mother

kasher: prepare food or vessels for use in a kosher home

kibbutz: collective farming community in Israel

kiddush: blessing sanctifying the Sabbath or holidays in the home or synagogue or refreshments accompanying such a ceremony

kippot: skullcaps (one: kippah)

kosher: foods prepared in accordance with religious law

kugel: pudding

l'hitraot (lehitraot): "till we meet again"; au revoir

latkes: pancakes, usually made with potatoes

lukshen: noodles

Medinat Yisrael: State of Israel

menorah: the seven-branched candelabrum, that was lighted daily in the Tabernacle and the Temple. Also called the *hanukkiah*, the eight-branched candelabrum, lighted for eight days, one candle added each day (see *hanukkiah)*

mitzvah: commandment; good deed

Mizpah: a *Mizpah* necklace made in the form of a pendant cut in two between the words "The Lord watch between me and thee, when we are absent one from another" (Genesis 31:49).

Saba: grandfather

Savta: grandmother

schnecken: German coffee cake

sedrah: weekly portion of the Torah, read on the Sabbath

Shabbat: Sabbath; Saturday; day of rest

Shabbat shalom: Sabbath greeting

shadchan: marriage-maker

shalom: peace; greeting: hello or good-bye

shammash: sexton of synagogue; ancillary candle used to light the others on the *hanukkiah*, pronouced "*shammes*" colloquially

shavua tov: a good week; greeting at end of Sabbath

shekel: basic coin of ancient and modern Israel; value today roughly one-half of a US dollar (during the time period of this book)

sherut: shared taxi

shuk: market-place

shul: synagogue (from German *schule*: school, place of learning)

Sim(c)hat Torah: holiday of Rejoicing of the Law

succah: temporary outside dwelling usually decorated with greens on top, where meals are eaten and time spent during Succot

Succot: Feast of Tabernacles; early fall harvest festival

Talmud: literally "instruction," usually refers to the authoritative body of Jewish tradition comprising the Mishnah and Gemara, which is post-biblical writings that contain legal, religious, ethical, historical and anecdotal material

Torah: literally, learning or law, usually refers to the covered scroll kept in the Holy Ark of the synagogue containing the Five Books of Moses

ushpizin: guests, usually referring to Biblical heroes invited on Succot (e.g. the Patriarchs, King David, Moses, etc.)

Yerushalayim: Jerusalem

yeshiva: Day school for intensive Jewish study, with a special focus on the Talmud

zemirot: songs sung at Sabbath and holidays meals

ABOUT THE AUTHOR

Benjamin Goodnick , PhD, ABPP, A"H, (1914-2011) pursued a career as a psychologist in the civilian and military fields. His experience included working in veterans' clinics, public, private and religious schools and private practice. His experience included serving as a leader in the Division of Special Education of Philadelphia. As chessed, he also gave of his time for psychological testing and counseling in the Jewish religious schools of the Philadelphia vicinity. However, his greatest joy and life dedication was in the establishment as a co-founder and later years of leadership as National Trustee and Philadelphia President of the Association of Orthodox Jewish Scientists.

His family lived on in his tradition, as his wife, Regina Perel A"H had a leadership role in Jewish communal and synagogue organizations. His daughter, Joan M. Westenholz PhD A"H served as creator, designer and Chief Curator of the Biblelands Museum of Jerusalem, Israel and also translated numerous texts from Akkadian (Ancient Babylonian) to English over the course of her life. His son, Paul J. Goodnick MD, carried on his tradition of caring in practice, teaching, and research over numerous years as a psychiatrist specializing in mood disorders, currently based at the Veterans Affairs Medical Center in New York City with an appointment to SUNY Downstate Medical School.

This work of fiction embodies the dedication of Dr. Benjamin Goodnick A"H to the importance of family and tradition in the pursuit of closeness to Hashem Above. This proximity leads to positive and wholesome outcomes overcoming times of challenge and bringing about possibilities in life of Hashem's hidden miracles in activities of our daily lives (*Neis Nistar*).